ALMOST A WISE GUY

(Based on a true story)

By

Fran Capo

Illustrated by

Vibhooshana

ISBN: 0-9724135-0-2

Library of Congress Control Number: 2002103506

This book is printed on acid free paper.

Printed in the United States of America
Bloomington, IN

What the readers are saying:

"**Fran Capo captures the real essence of growing up in NYC--the sense of humor needed for living and working the New York "streets". "Almost A Wise Guy" is a real winner, full of warmth, truth, and humor."**
- Joey Novick
President, Flemington Borough Council
Flemington, NJ

"**Very funny down to earth neighborhood story. I give it four cannolis**"
-Vincent M. Gogliormella
Creator of the Broadway comedy hit
Six Goumbas and a Wannabe.

"**Great character. Great story. Has all the makings for a great screenplay.**"
-Heidi Adam
Emmy award winning producer

"**I didn't do all those things! Well...maybe.**"
-Rose Capo (*Fran's mom*)

Dedication

To My Dear Ole Dad, Frank
Who always made me feel protected,
taught me how to fight, look at the bottom line,
tell a good story, that there was a solution to
any problem and above all to laugh in any situation.
I love you Dad —
wouldn't trade you for the world.

Author's note:

The author assumes no liability for accidents happening to, or injuries sustained by, readers who engage in the activities described in this book.

The names in this story have been changed... to protect the author.

Some of the characters are based on real people. Some are not. Chances are if you think you know the person it's purely coincidental. Then again maybe it's not.

Special thanks to:

My wonderful boyfriend, Steve, who believed in the potential of this book so much, he financed it, without a contract! Thanks, I love you.

My partner in *The Estrogen Files* and good friend, Anna Collins, for doing a first read on my book and giving it the once over.

My editor, Charlene Patterson, who always is so positive and supportive in all my work.

My forever understanding son, Spencer who gives up countless hours of our time together so I can get my work done.

My mom, who taught me nothing is impossible and to always go for my dreams.

Alexander Palacios for being the stand-in model for the cover of the book.

Vibhooshana Heiden for doing such a wonderful job on the cover and being such a great spirit to work with.

Steve Heiden for the great job on the type face and for coming through, and delaying his holiday plans.

Dan Heise and Charles Higgins at 1st books for answering my numerous questions.

The production team for making all the changes requested.

Cindy Baker for putting my book up on the website.

Tony Giannone for his wonderful talent, and for my sister, Shahira for recommending him.

If there is anyone else I left out, I'll save that for my speech at the Emmy's!

Foreword

Growing up, I remember bits and pieces of things my dad told me. I also remember how my dad would disappear for a while. I thought he was working on some big out-of-state construction job, later to find out he was doing stints in jail. As I grew older I learned more about his world, but he always told me about it in a funny way, I guess so he wouldn't worry my sister and me.

My dad hung around some pretty shady characters, always had a unique way of looking at things, and a lot of times they weren't legit. Whenever he would try to get me involved in one of his scams he'd be offended that I wouldn't go along with them. He'd say, "Aw, you ain't my daughter, you sure you're a Capo?" Then laugh.

But his underlying theme was always: find the humor in life, no matter what you do. This philosophy is why I became a stand-up comic. From my mom I learned nothing was impossible and always to face a challenge when it appeared.

When my dad was in the fourth stage of cancer, he was still joking around. By then I was an author. My dad pulled me aside and asked me if I would write the story of his life, including all his crazy escapades. He told me, "I even have the name of the book, 'Almost a Wise Guy.'"

It was an offer I couldn't refuse. For the next few months I taped the stories my dad told. Every time I would ask for details he'd say, "This was many years ago, you expect me to remember everything?" So often I would rely on newspaper clippings about his illegal escapades that he had stashed away. Sometimes I'd ask my mom for information, but she had a totally different take on the stories. Then I'd ask my uncle to verify some facts, to which he'd reply, "This is many years ago, you expect me to remember everything?"

Whatever wasn't remembered, my dad reasoned, "You're the author, that's where you come in; use poetic license." And so some stories became embellished to fill in the gaps. Thus this book is BASED on a true story, and not the whole story, so help me God.

I raced desperately to write the book, edit it, and read it to my father so he could hear the finished project before he died. I wrote the book in a few months. I read a chapter to him every night as I finished it. After hearing the whole book, he smiled, nodded his head, and said, "Good, now what's next?" Next? I was angry. What are you talking about? It's done.

"Don't you have to get it published or talk to the powers that be so people can read the story?" My mind was racing. Did I want people knowing the world's fastest talking female's dad was almost a wise guy? Worse yet, did I want some mobster guy coming after me, the FBI tailing me to see if I knew anything else, or relatives coming up to me at the next family picnic and asking, "How come you didn't mention me?" The truth is, I think some of my friends thought my dad was in the mob anyway, considering the family name.

I thought hard about this. Mmmm, I loved him, the story was interesting and funny, but I wasn't really ready to let the world know. Then the writer in me took over and said, "Compromise Capo." So, I decided to change some names and pretend it was a novel.

A few years have passed since my dad died. I'm keeping my word and publishing his story. I've also decided that, if I'm to live the philosophy I always teach in my motivational lectures then I have to be true to myself, have a good time, and "Fear Nothing."

The truth is, my dad did live this life, and if one day I'm really going to become famous or decide to run for political office, it's going to come out anyway, so why not now, straight from the horse's mouth, more or less?

So here it is, the story of Frankie Crooks, my dad, who was Almost a Wise Guy...

Chapter One

I had the best of both worlds. Connections on both sides of the fence. Two brothers, one a cop as straight as they come and highly decorated, the other involved in the mob. I was the youngest. I admired both of them, so naturally I was caught in the middle, like the cream of an Oreo cookie.

You wanna know what it was like darting in and out of a life a crime, where something so small creates a domino effect and before you know it you're in so deep you can't see the shore and you're not sure you remember how to swim? Where you have a devil on your left shoulder and an angel on the right and they're both whispering "I've got the money." I'll tell you a story...sit down. Frankie Crooks the name, on account that I got a bent arm, but I guess the other meaning could fit too.

1

Growing up my mom, a short, thin, dark Italian woman who could manage with the English language but not read a word of it, God rest her soul, didn't have a clue. Mom hated the name Crooks and I constantly had to reassure her that it was 'cause of my arm. But mothers aren't stupid; they selectively choose to be blind and clueless.

Now you gotta remember, this was sixty years ago. My mom, Mary, was a mail order bride. One day my dad wrote home to Italy that he couldn't find a decent woman here in America, so he asked his family if they could please send him a bride and some pastries. My mom arrived with a dowry and a box of authentic Italian pastries under her arm. What a deal. I guess it's not much different than the personals today, except you don't get cannolis. As she stepped onto American soil, she spotted her future, my dad, John. They exchanged greetings, then she was swept away to a friend's house for a week till they got married by a

2

justice of the peace. She moved in with Dad and became the Mrs., just like that.

I wish I could say it was love at first sight, but it wasn't. They did make a good team, and in those days that was important. Shortly after they married, my mom began working in a factory on West Broadway, making artificial flowers. She'd come home everyday smelling like plastic roses—a smell I grew to love.

My dad, a tough looking Neapolitan who became a U.S. Citizen after he was drafted into the Army just a few weeks after stepping onto American soil, was stocky, had a big face with deep, inset lines, brown eyes, and was very serious. He would get up every morning at five o'clock and go through his morning body cleansing, which entailed clearing his throat a thousand times and then farting loudly, a smell I grew to hate, but an art I grew to perfect. Then he would take a train into New Jersey to work in a dye factory. Every night he'd come home with a different color dye embedded in the cracks of his leathery hands. Both my parents were Italian immigrants working hard to raise a family. I wanted to do better.

We lived in the Village at 141 Sullivan Street. We were on the fourth floor. The apartment was painted puke green with a ceramic tub in the kitchen—the type with claw legs—and a bathroom in the hallway outside the apartment that we had to share with our neighbors. Made for one strong bladder. We had a black pot belly stove that heated the house and also served as our room deodorizer. My dad used to throw orange peels on top of the stove, and as they slowly baked, the whole apartment would have that Airwick cardboard tree cutout smell. Many years later I used to buy those off of street vendors and stick them in my car. They reminded me of home.

It was one of those twenty-dollars-a-month, cold water, flat, railroad apartments where you have to go through every room to get to yours, especially if it happened to be the last one like mine was. Well, it really wasn't "my" room; I shared it with three others. My older brothers, Vinny and Joey, and our mutt, Butch. My sister, Teresa, had her own room since she was the only girl. Them's the breaks. I, of course, was the baby of the family.

Teresa was my protector and the one I got into the most trouble with as a kid. She was always plotting some Lucille Ball-type scheme with me as Ethel—the stooge. I remember one time in grammar school my sister wanted to see Frank Sinatra, and I was supposed to be her alibi.

"Come on, Frankie, tell your teacher you're not feeling well. Then I'll come pick you up since Ma's at work and we'll cut out and see the concert."

I was a little hesitant since I had been playing sick a lot lately to hangout with my friends. But it was my sister, so I agreed. I went into the classroom and started moaning.

"What is it now, Frankie?!" the teacher snapped.

"My stomach hurts real bad. I think I'm gonna puke." She looked at me suspiciously. I had to up the ante. So I started making those dry heave sounds, like a cat does when it's spitting up a hairball. It worked, the teacher panicked.

"Go to the bathroom! I'll call your sister," she screamed.

I ran to the bathroom laughing all the way. I waited a few minutes to let her summon my sister. The plan was going as scheduled. My teacher and sister stood in the hall talking. I casually strolled over, pretending I was unaware of their little discussion. Then the teacher laid it on me from left field.

"Teresa, it seems as if you're little brother here has been feeling sick a lot lately. Take him to your family doctor. I want to see a note that explains what's the matter," she said matter-of-factly. Teresa nodded, and we walked out of hearing range of the teacher. Sis then turned to me as if possessed. "You had to overact, didn't you!?" Then she smacked me on the head. I just smirked and shrugged.

We hadn't counted on this. My sister took me over to the doctor's. I didn't want to go, but we had to get that stupid note.

To make matters worse, while we were waiting in the doctor's office, the nurse said we had to contact my mom, since Teresa was not my legal guardian. So the nurse rang up my mom, and the doctor took me into the examination room. My sister, embarrassingly enough, volunteered to come into the room with me, probably to make sure I didn't blow our cover.

"What seems to be the trouble, Frankie?" the doc asked.

"Nothing really, Doc." Then I get an elbow from Teresa.

"He's been having stomach pains. He's just trying to be a big shot." She gave me those big eyes...as if to say "play along stupid."

"Yeah, yeah...a little pain here and there," I reluctantly replied.

"Does it hurt here?" Doc continued.

"No," I said.

"Here?"

"No."

"Here?" He looked like he was getting annoyed. My sister must have sensed this, and she sent me another one of those "I'll kill you" looks.

"Yes. Yeah," I said. Well, of all the damn places, I had pin-marked my appendix. Great! By this time my mom had arrived all worried and smelling like plastic flowers.

"Oh my little Frankie!" she cried.

The doctor took her aside with Teresa and whispered. A doctor whispering is never a good sign.

"What? What!" I say.

"I'm afraid, son, you have to have your appendix out."

"Appendix!" Hey, I was only kidding. Teresa, tell him we were just joking." Teresa just stared dumbly, innocent as all hell.

"Now don't be scared, son. It's better we take it out now, or it can burst." The doctor was firm but kind in an ironic way.

"Burst! Ma, I feel okay, really."

"Don't you argue with the doctor, Frankie. I'll be right here." Then she turned to Teresa. "Teresa, you a good girl for bringing your brother. Now go. Go!" And my mother scooted her off.

Good girl my ass! I saw a gleam in Teresa's eyes. She looked over her shoulder back at me and shrugged. Meanwhile, I was desperately trying to convince my

9

mother I was okay, and she thought I was turning into some kind of a crybaby. I was fighting to save a part of me that ain't broke, to keep me as one, and mom was trying to comfort me. I suddenly knew how Columbus must have felt saying the world was round with a hundred sailors saying, "Yeah, Chris, I'll wait for you at the edge." No matter how I pleaded, the result was the knife. The kick was Sister dear went to the concert and was busy swooning at old Blue Eyes while all I got was a big two inch scar where my appendix used to be. To this day that scar reminds me of her. No hard feelings, though. Win some. Lose some. That's the way the cookie crumbles.

As a teen I got into my own trouble. The one thing you had to learn early in my neighborhood was how to be sneaky. Before talk of Big Brother ever came about, my neighborhood had Big Mama. Everyone kept their doors and eyes open. You couldn't do anything because everyone in the neighborhood knew who you were. If you did something bad, your mother heard about it through the village grapevine, which traveled faster than paper through a shredder in the White House. Then you'd get the crap beat out of you with a broom, or shoe, or whatever happened to be in her hand at the time. This was 1946, child abuse laws weren't around. Besides, you didn't want to call the cops on your parents, because they'd beat the crap out of you, too, for not listening to your parents in the first place.

I still hated school, so I cut as often as I could. The teachers never gave me too much of a hassle. I think they thought I was hopeless. Plus, it helped that they thought I looked like a short Elvis. I was more scared of my mother. I had to find a place to hangout so the neighbors wouldn't see me. Cutting school wasn't so bad; the only thing that suffered was my spelling. But who gave a crap—that's what secretaries are for. The important stuff, the real life survival stuff, I learned on the outside.

My first encounter with the mob was purely by accident. A friend of mine named Eddie Finger asked me if I wanted to shoot some pool at the Lexington Avenue Social Club. I had heard of the club. It was an invitation-only organization and was about as social as a pitbull in heat, but I was game. I had learned how to shoot pool at the Police Athletic League thanks to my brother Joey. Joey was always on the up and up. He wore a clean military cut and was lean and quick with a joke. He was the most honest guy I ever knew. He would have cringed if he had known where I was about to sport my talent.

Eddie, a tall kid, about six foot two, with dark curly hair and a spoon-shaped scar on his jaw two inches wide, knocked three times on the unmarked steel door with his eggplant-sized hands. He waited, then knocked again twice. We got in, no sweat. The place

12

was dark and dingy. A thick layer of smoke hung over the room like a cheap toupee. Everyone smoked back then, that was the thing to do. It made you look cool. No one knew about that second-hand smoke crap, and if they did, they were tough guys, so they would have ignored it anyway.

Some older guys were just hanging around drinking espresso and reading the paper. A wooden bar lined the left wall of the place with two overhead Tiffany lights. I knew they were Tiffany 'cause my mom always wanted to get a light like them. That was for rich people, though. The bartender looked like he'd seen better days. He was just smoking a cigar and gazing out, nervously cleaning a glass as he did. He was missing a finger. I looked at Eddie. He grinned. "He used to point, so it got cut off." Eddie had a temper. They didn't call him Finger for nothing.

The bartender glanced at me suspiciously but said nothing. I think he valued his other nine digits. The two pool tables were at the far end of the room.

Eddie racked up with a cigarette dangling from his mouth and his eyes all squinty from the smoke. Eddie was the type of kid you couldn't trust, but he was in with a lot of people, so he was a good person to know. He always looked mean. He had to, especially after he got that stupid-looking scar on his face. Everyone thought it was the butt end of a police gun that caused it. At least that's what Eddie told them. I knew better. A friend of mine lived next door to Eddie and told me what happened. One night Eddie told his mom her meatballs were soggy. She started screaming and yelling and wailed a hot metal spoon at him from across the room. It whacked him on the face. The edge of the spoon ripped into his jaw. It was one of those freak accidents that leaves you scarred for life. Ever since then Eddie always acted mean. I also heard he never ate meatballs again.

Anyway, we started to shoot. Soon I was caught up in the moment. So there I was hanging out at the pool hall perfecting my game. I was sixteen at the time, had just started to smoke, and was cutting school as usual. Eddie was eighteen, the legal age to play. I was getting ready to sink the eight ball off three rails into the corner pocket, a shot I'd done hundreds of times, when all of a sudden I felt a swift kick in the ass. Without looking, I swung my pool cue to hit the perpetrator. I missed and left a nice knick in the wall with the butt end of the cue. I looked around. Everyone was staring at me, ready to lunge and attack. I was a stranger in this place. Even Eddie looked like he wanted to kill me. I dropped the cue and bolted out the door. I ran like the wind down Lexington, checking to see if I was being chased. Running was another thing I'd perfected. I could hit fast and run like a demon.

15

When I got home my brother Vinny came into my room and grabbed me by the scruff of the neck. When Vinny grabbed you, you knew it. He was built like a bulldog, five foot seven, round faced, and gruff, with short arms and legs. Vice-grip Vin, he'd squish you like a gnat. "You're in trouble, kid. Come with me and don't say nothin." I was shitting in my pants. Vinny had a whole other grapevine at work.

As we were walking, my brother said, "Do you know what you did today?"

"Yeah, I played pool and some schmuck kicked me in the ass. I tried to hit him, but I missed so I ran."

"You jerk. You know who that schmuck was?" Vinny's voice was steady but angry. I was about to answer, but his look told me to keep quiet. "That schmuck was Mario Gendarmo," he continued. "You pissed off the big man."

At the time, the Gendarmos were the big crime family, and Mario was the Capo di tutti. "Vin, I didn't know," I uttered.

We arrived back at the pool hall. Vinny led me to a back room. He knocked, and an eyeball darted around a peephole and let us in. Entering this back room was like being transformed into another world—chandeliers, spitshine floor, plush couches, some delicious pasta reeking of garlic simmering in their eat-in kitchen next to a fully stocked marble bar.

Five giants stood guarding Mario Gendarmo and his espresso. He just stared at us. His eyes were cold and piercing. I had heard ruthless stories about him but had never met the man face to face, and this was definitely not the ideal situation.

My brother spoke: "Mr. Gendarmo, this is my brother, Frankie Crooks. He didn't know who you were, sir. He never would have done it. My brother just swung by instinct to cover himself. He's a good kid, just a little stunad sometimes." That comment hurt, but I wasn't about to correct him and prove him right.

Mario Gendarmo just nodded and leaned forward. He motioned with a quick nod for me to approach him. I felt like David without the slingshot. I walked up to the table and mumbled, "I'm sorry, Mr. Gendarmo. I shouldn't have been here. I'll never come back unless I have your permission."

Mario Gendarmo just nodded, gave an odd grin, waved his hand, and said to my brother, "Take care of him." Oh man, my brother was going to whack me. Moma would be pissed. We went outside. Vinny shoved me ahead of him.

Once we were outside the pool hall Vinny looked me straight in the eyes. I'd never seen him so mad. "I'm supposed to smack you around a bit and teach you a lesson. I'm going let you slide. Don't be an ass. Wise up. Watch who you're swinging at. Next time you might not be so lucky."

It was then that I learned the silent code of the families. If you don't know who "someone's with"—which family they are in with—and you have a run in, they let you slide. But if you know which family they are with, and you don't go through the proper channels to amend any conflicts, then kiss your ass good-bye.

Both my ignorance and my brother Vinny's connections saved me. Trying to slug the biggest man in the biggest crime family was definitely tempting fate.

I was thankful yet in awe of the power that one man could have with the wave of a hand. Scared, yet intrigued. I was strangely drawn to this side of the world. At that moment I decided...I wanted to become a wise guy.

Chapter Two

I was sixteen and needed a driver's license. I was a smart guy always looking for an angle. I devised the perfect plan, one that looked good on the outside, got me what I wanted and no one got hurt.

I became an altar boy at St. Mary's of Perpetual Sin. This church was kind of like the last stop for wayward boys. They needed altar and choir boys. Since my singing sounded like Yoko Ono on a bad hair day, I decided to opt for the altar boy. The duties were simple: Come on Sundays to help the priest with the bread and wine, do a few chores, and help with some office duties and rituals. That last part attracted my eye.

I went to Father Jim and applied for the position. My mom, God rest her soul, was thrilled. Her son an altar boy. Something for the nosy neighbors who were always trying to figure out what my brother Vinny was into to chew on.

One neighbor, Mrs. Mahoney, was always snooping around. She was a short, fat woman with a butt the size of Idaho. Why are the nosy ones always homely? She'd come around with some brownies or fresh-baked bread, always peering over my mom's shoulder to see what "stolen goods" might be in the house. She never found nothin', 'cause there was nothin' to find. Vinny never brought his work home. We were poor, yet Vinny always had a new car and a wad of money. I overheard her talking to a neighbor one day, saying that she thought something fishy was going on. Vinny didn't give a rat's ass. He felt it was his life and he'd do with it what he damn well pleased. Besides, he had nothing to hide. He brought good money into the family. I loved his attitude: Don't care what anyone thinks, just do what you gotta do for the family.

21

Anyway, I had to go to church three times a week. I went right after school, or when school was supposedly over, because sometimes I cut.

St. Mary's was a big, old church—the kind that smelled holy but also gave you the creeps, like some old priests or nuns might be buried below the floors. At any given time you could walk in there and see a couple of old folks on their knees praying or lighting candles for the miracles they needed. I always hoped they got what they prayed for. God's good that way. He can listen to a million people at the same time and not need call waiting.

Some people complain that God doesn't answer their prayers. I believe God is alive, but sometimes he just doesn't want to get involved. Either way, people always showed up in church, just in case.

About two hundred and fifty people could fit easily into the pews to listen to a Sunday sermon and try to redeem their souls before mere mortal temptations took over. I guess I should have gone to more sermons.

Until my altar boy days, I had only seen the public side of the church. The wooden pews, the stained glass windows showing the slow death of Jesus, the omnipotent altar, and the cross bearing Jesus with INRI at the top. I always wondered why they didn't show Jesus chowing down at the last supper to remind us of the good things in life, not the death to remind us he died for our sins. But I guess we all need a good kick in the butt to keep us in place. Don't get me wrong, I am really religious and I believe in God like I said. It's just that sometimes I wish religion was more cheerful. But whether you're a good guy or bad guy, fear is power.

The confessionals area was the place I liked the most. The concept is simple. You go in this dark, closetlike box and kneel down. Then, after a few opening words, "Bless me Father for I have sinned," you drop your evils and misdoings for the week in the box, come out, say a few prayers, and you're absolved. You speak to a priest through a little window so neither of you have to face each other. In that box you can bare your soul to the servant of God and be free, unless of course guilt kicks in. I think I'd be a lot more scared if my mother and father were in that box and heard what I had to say. They were a lot harder on me than the Big Guy. I was told God has a way of forgiving us all, not like us mere mortals who can hold grudges forever. Anyway, I hoped it was really true since I figured after my altar boy caper I'd be spending a lot of time in that box. Maybe even have to order in a pizza.

Father Jim and I became very close. He would let me carry his long, red robe, which was a privilege. Meant he really trusted me. I'd go to his office, a plain wood-paneled room with a typewriter, desk, lots of holy pictures and books all around, file cabinets, all the ritual papers and the seal. The one thing that cracked me up was a picture of the Pope shaking hands with Frank Sinatra. Something very funny about that, but I guess we all liked "Ole Blue Eyes" at the time. I touched my scar on my stomach in salute.

I watched very closely when I was in his office, taking a mental note of the objects in the room, as I'd need to get in and out very quickly when the time was right.

Father Jim was down to earth. I really liked him. He was in his mid-thirties, a good-looking Irish guy I guess, in good shape, and soft spoken. I couldn't picture him being anything but a priest. You really have to have strong beliefs to swear off women.

I felt conflict about what I was going to do—my big plan—but I thought in the long run, he really wouldn't mind. He probably did some stupid things in his life, too, before he turned to God. The way I see it, no one really has a clear conscience, they usually just have a bad memory.

I was an altar boy for six months before the opportunity hit. In the meantime, I learned all my prayers, some Latin phrases, and did a lot of chores for the church. It was kind of cool being the center of attention on Sundays. All eyes were upon you. You're there hoping you don't screw up and hand him the wine instead of the bread or something stupid like that.

I remember one time Father Jim approached me in the back of the church. I had learned all the names of the parts of the ceremony and I was trying really hard to impress the Father. He started talking to me, saying, "Son you are doing a great job. Do you remember all the words and things needed for Mass?"

"Yes, Father," I quickly replied.

"Good. Now then, get me the steps."

I just stared at him thinking, "The steps? The steps? What the heck are the steps?" Is that the steps

Jesus took to the cross, no that's the stations. I was racking my brain and I guess I stood there too long.

He looked down on me and said, "Frankie, get me the steps please."

I started to stutter, "I'm sorry father...I don't remember..."

"Frankie!" he yelled. "Get me the ladder!"

Boy did I feel like an asshole.

Anyway, my family always sat in the first row. My dad always had a stern look on his face. My sister, Teresa, sat in the middle always twiddling with her jet black hair. My two brothers poked at each other, and my mom always smiled at me. My mom really loved me. I could see it in her eyes. I was the baby boy, her little Frankie. All right, my mom spoiled me rotten, and I loved it.

I remember one Sunday Father Jim is talking about giving good to the world and it will give it back to you.

Today they call it karma. I call it getting what you deserve. I believe that.

The congregation was only half full that day. Father Jim was passionately, yet softly, telling the people to give love first, then love will follow. The problem was there were not enough people to hear his message. After his sermon, he looked a bit discouraged. He asked me to go to his office and get a baptismal certificate that he needed for a two o'clock Baptism. He said, "I trust you with the keys. I wish more kids your age would come to the church." I assured him in time they would. Just don't give up.

I walked down the stairs and into the long, lonely corridor to his office. Everyone was upstairs in the church. I unlocked the door to his office. So quiet. It felt as if I had stepped onto holy ground. Everything was just as I remembered it. I clicked on the light and there was Frank Sinatra grinning down at me. Then I said, "Act cool, Frankie. Father Jim gave you permission to be here."

I went into his desk and got out the baptismal papers. This was my chance. I had the keys, I had the big guy's permission to be in his desk, and right in front of me were hundreds of blank certificates not numbered. Payday. How many should I take? Just a few...he'll never notice. My hands were beginning to sweat since I couldn't tell how long I'd been gone and I didn't want him to come after me to find out what had happened. I started talking to myself, "Think, Crooks, think." Okay, I'll take them. I've waited six months for this opportunity. Something has to be said for patience. I quickly stamped a few certificates with the seal, blew the ink dry, and was ready to leave.

Now, where to hide the damn things? I tucked them flat against my back, held securely in by my pants. The altar boy maternity robe covered it. I prayed I wouldn't sweat and smear the ink. How ironic, here I am praying to God for his help in committing a crime in his own house.

I clicked out the lights, locked the door, and went over to Father Jim and handed him a single sheet of baptismal paper. "Thanks, Frankie, nice job." For a second, a pang of guilt shot through me. I thought I felt the papers stab me in the back. "Nice job?" What did he mean? Did he know? Of course not.

The Baptism went off without a hitch. The baby screamed as usual, as the water was poured over his head. The parents beamed, pictures were taken, and in an hour or so it was over. I spent the time daydreaming, watching everything as if it were a silent film. The only words I could later remember were "release this child from original sin." That echoed in my ears and lingered for a while.

Outside the church I made sure no one was looking before I pulled the certificates from my pants. The top one had smeared, but I could salvage the rest. I tucked them back in and ran home.

As I ran, it really hit me. I'd committed my first crime, and it was against a priest. Was I nuts? Talk about a one-way ticket to Hell. But I couldn't think about that now, the adrenaline was still pumping. Besides, I now had my ticket to a driver's license. I forged the priest's name on the papers, wrote in a date of birth earlier than my own, and, bingo, I was eighteen. I had taken ten certificates in all. Later I sold them to my friends for ten dollars a pop. Nice little profit. I had taken a little and shared with my friends. We all were happy.

I never went back to St. Mary's of Perpetual Sin.

A couple of times I thought about telling Father Jim, but then he'd make me give the papers back, and that would defeat the whole purpose. I was sorry I sneaked behind Father Jim's back, but I was happy I had my driver's license. It was a double edged sword, but for now I didn't feel too bad. I was kind of proud of myself for having the guts to do it

I told my mother and father I had to quit being an altar boy because I got a night job and that I wanted to save for a car. This was partially true. Vinny knew the score. I was winning money shooting pool at night and wanted to hangout with my friends. The money was good but not enough to get a car as fast as I wanted. Of course, there were always other ways.

Chapter Three

Vinny always came in late from who knows where. My mom and dad never questioned him, which always annoyed me to no end. I made the mistake of telling my mom that my job ended at midnight. If I came in a few minutes late, it was like the Spanish Inquisition. But I guess the fact that Vin was bringing in a lot of money and was the oldest gave him that privilege. My mom thought he was some big shot business man, always dressed in expensive suits. She was proud of her oldest son.

Since he got in late, he slept late. I took advantage of this. I used to take his keys out of his pocket on weekends and drive his car.

He had a shiny battleship-gray Caddie complete with all the trimmings: leather seats, radio, big silver hood ornament, and a horn that sounded like "Get your ass out of my way." Not some wimpy, high-pitched "beep beep" horn that would belong to a science nerd with a pocket protector. Everyday he parked the car in the same spot. Kind of like a wolf that marks off his territory. No one in the neighborhood would ever take that spot. Only some jerk checking out the Village and doing a tourist thing might consider it not knowing the consequences.

As soon as my brother Joey left, I'd get up and sneak the keys out of Vinny's pants. I'd have to toss Butch a bone to keep him quiet, and then I'd run down four flights of stairs and go to my secret hiding place underneath the stairwell where I kept four cinder blocks.

I'd go out to the car, double-park it for a few seconds, and then place the cinder blocks in the spot so no one would take it. Then I was off.

I loved riding in Vinny's car. I felt like a big shot, and it didn't do too bad for my image with the girls. I'd ride on the safe streets like Sullivan, not Thompson.

Thompson Street had all the pushcarts lined up where everyone would sell their stuff from fruits to undershirts. There were hordes of loud people bargaining for prices and exchanging the latest gossip.

I'd drive past the stable and poultry shop where I could hear the caged chickens every morning. Those chickens were loud. I guess I'd be too if I was on death row. One time I had to hit the breaks when a headless chicken got away and was coming straight for me. Not as intimidating as the headless horseman, but I hit the brakes none the less. It died in front of the car. Some say it had a heart attack, I say it was because he lost his head. Okay... it's a stupid joke. Quit your moaning.

Anyway, since I didn't try to hide the fact that I was driving Vinny's car, everyone thought he'd lent it to me. They say the best way to hide something is to put it right in front of the person's nose. So that's what I did. Waving to everyone and saying good morning. It was a sweet deal. I'd drive around for about an hour, and I always replaced the gas and got back in time to let the engine cool down.

Then one day as I pulled into Sullivan Street and went to park, I saw a dirty, broken-down Ford in my brother's spot. The cinder blocks had been tossed on the side of the curb. "I'm dead," I thought. I double-parked the car and tried to locate the owner. I figured I could beg for sympathy. But I couldn't find the guy anywhere. I had to park Vinny's car a block away.

I was nervous. I ran upstairs and looked out the front window. I kept the keys in my pocket; if by some miracle the moron would move his car I could bolt and put it back in its rightful spot. No such luck.

I heard Vinny get up. This was it. The first thing he did every morning was look out the window and check his car. I tried to stall fate. I started asking him questions and told him I needed some advice on women. He knew I was lying. That deadly second of silence occurred, just before an eminent explosion. He pushed me out of the way. "Where the hell's my car? Did you see someone steal it?"

Then I did the only thing I could to salvage my butt. I blurted out, "I took your car for a ride and parked it around the block." Then I ran like hell down the hall yelling, "Ma! Vinny's gonna kill me." He was right on my tail. My mom stopped him dead in his tracks. "Don't you hurta my little Frankie. I breaka you face." Then she whacked him on the head.

My brother protested. "But Ma, he drove my car without asking, and he's underage." Then she turned around and said, "Not my little Frankie."

Feeling a little too cocky I said, "See Vinny. Listen to Moma." She whirled around and all ninety-two pounds of her whacked me.

"Don't you ever lie to your moma." Now we were even. Thank God she didn't have a spoon in her hand.

That out of the way, I still needed my own set of wheels.

As luck would have it, my bad grades paid off. I got sent to the last stop on the educational train...Chelsea Vocational. The place where they sent all underage kids who got thrown out of every other school. The perfect training ground. My favorite class was auto mechanics, taught by Mr. Bennett. Bennett was a tall man with soldier-cut white hair and biceps as big as scuba tanks. He fancied himself some closet marine and would bark orders out to us: "I'll give you boys exactly one minute and twenty-eight seconds to change those tires or you'll drop and give me ten." It was like training for the Indie 500. I think he thought he could reform us "bad" boys. The only reason we did it was because we had other plans.

It was at Chelsea that I learned how to hotwire a car. In those days it was simple. You just had to get under the hood. There were two screws for ignition. You'd get a pair of jumper wires, match the ignition wires to the screws, and, bingo, start up the engine.

This was a move we practiced over and over again. Me and my friend Johnny Rizzo could do it in our sleep. We had a lot in common; we were both in the market for a car.

Then the opportunity struck. As Rizzo and I were leaving school one day we noticed Mr. Bennett's army-green Chevy with a decal of the American Flag on the driver's window parked alongside the school. We also noticed that he'd conveniently left the keys in the ignition. You would think the Colonel would have known better. We felt it our job to teach him a lesson. He wouldn't know it was missing for hours, because he still had more classes to teach. Rizzo asked, "Wanna take it?" In an instant we knew we would. I hopped in the drivers seat. The damn seat was stuck all the way back because of Bennett's tall legs. I practically had to hug the wheel to floor the gas. We peeled out of that spot.

We cruised around town taking turns driving. We obeyed all traffic laws so as not to arouse suspicion. Remember it's all in the attitude. If you act as if you own the place, they don't even look twice. "Do it in the open," was my motto. So with attitude, we drove all the way up to Dobbs Ferry, a good forty-five minute ride from Manhattan. We even stopped and ate at Scapi's, a local combination pizza place and bowling alley. Great pizza and cheap bowling—need I say more? You could play all day for a twenty-five cents. Of course, in those days you had to set up your own pins. Kind of like self-service bowling. If you really wanted to have fun, you would throw the ball while your friends were setting up the pins and watch 'em run.

With pizza bellies we drove back to Manhattan. On the way back we were cruising along Riverside Drive enjoying our borrowed car, listening to the radio, trying to figure out where to dump the car when all of a sudden...BOOM! I smashed into the side of this guy's brand new Cadillac. This jerk had just pulled out of a parking spot, no signal, nothin. I caught the Caddie in the left front panel and the metal jammed into his wheel. As we got out of the car, the guy's tire went flat. The final insult.

You don't know fear till you're in a stolen Chevy owned by a wannabe marine and have just hit a brand new car. The guy's car was badly damaged, but Bennett's tank was untouched. We got out of Bennett's car, and before we even had shut the door, Danny Devito's stunt double started reading us the riot act. "You idiots!!! Where the hell are your eyes? Staring up your asshole! My brand new car...look at it! You jerkoffs!" On and on with words I'd never heard in the Bible. He started turning red and yelling for a policeman. "Just you wait, you delinquents! You're gonna need a lot of money to cover this, boys." The fat man screamed. Rizzo and I looked at each other; no one was around. We looked at the guy, this Pillsbury doughboy with an attitude. I belted the guy and we ran for our lives. As we ran, we heard distant curses. We caught the nearest bus and went home.

The next day in class Rizzo and I had on our best poker faces as Bennett told the class about the stolen car. He threatened to break the neck of whatever punk had taken it. After class I went up to Bennett. "Look Mr. Bennett, I have a few friends that can ask around and see what happened to your car. Things like this travel." He grinned at me with a glimpse of suspicion and said, "Thanks, Frankie. Just keep your nose clean and stay out of trouble. Let the police handle this. They'll dust the car for fingerprints and catch the hoodlums."

"Can they do that?" I asked casually.

"Sure they can. I've seen it done myself." He smiled and turned away. I thought, nah, he's just bluffing. But just in case, I decided that if I ever did anything like this again, I would wear gloves, no matter how stupid I looked.

I'm not sure if it was my acting or lady luck, but we never got caught. I guess dough boy couldn't remember our faces and Bennett wasn't such a bad guy, although he did seem to be watching us more carefully for the next few days.

Bennett got his car back two weeks later unharmed except for a few extra miles. I decided that stealing a car was stupid and wasn't worth the risk. There was no money involved, and why go to jail for a joy ride? I had better things to do. From now on, I'd only do things that would turn a profit...I was in it for the money.

Chapter Four

Chelsea Vocational turned out to be an all around training ground. My hygiene teacher, Mr. Hornsman, was an ex-golden glove boxer. I think that must have been the requirement for teachers at Chelsea: The hell with their degree, how much crowd control could they could do?

Looking at Hornsman you never would have known he knew how to fight. He looked mild-mannered, kind of like the Clark Kent type, glasses and all. I could sense under that nerdish facade was a kick-ass kind of guy. Mr. Hornsman had observed me in the gym. He knew I was fast with my hands and quick with my feet. He wanted discipline in his class, and he was used to getting it with his hands. He was a delinquent in his youth himself. He told us a couple of stories, but no one in the class believed him. Regardless, in the classroom he had to use words. He couldn't punch out students, no matter how bad they were. But I could. And that's exactly the deal Mr. Hornsman cut with me.

He pulled me aside one day after class. "Frankie, I like you, but you're not the smartest student. Don't get me wrong, I think you have a lot of other things going for you. Listen, I feel I can trust you and make your mom happy at the same time. I'll give you straight A's if you straighten out any student in my class that doesn't listen. I don't wanna know about it, and don't do nothin' that will get the police involved. Deal?"

I shrugged, held out my hand, and said, "Deal."

It worked out fine for me. At first I couldn't figure out why Mr. Hornsman would approach me with such an offer. If the principal of the school found out that the only "by the book" teacher in his school was doing this, I was sure he'd get canned or at least in some serious trouble. I guess Hornsman knew I'd never tell and that any of the kids that would rat on me for setting them straight would get quickly quieted by a right hook.

It wasn't until my second semester that I realized Hornsman had plans for me. He wanted to train me as a boxer and be my manager. I agreed to fight for the school's boxing team. It was on the level and okay with the Board of Ed. One, because they didn't give a rat's ass about our school and figured if we beat up on each other we'd leave the "good kids" alone, and two, the matches brought money into the school. After all, this wasn't the type of school that would raise money on the local cake sale.

Besides, in a school of tough kids, the fights made me look good. And outside of school the boxing made me extra cash in illegal fights, a nice side income to my gambling. It was a win–win situation.

My first legitimate fight took place at St. Anthony's on Thompson Street. I was up against this kid named Tony Ginone. Tony was scared of me before he got into the ring, so it was an easy fight. In any sport, a lot of it is mental. If you psyche out your opponent, you've already won half the battle. Another bit of pre-fight advice that Mr. Hornsman told me that stuck was, "Always believe in yourself and always hit first. When you go out there, think about the hardest punch you can, then use it, wham...and scare your opponent."

I came out with a upper cut to his jaw. Tony's head snapped back like a cap on a shaken bottle of coke. Fear flashed in his eyes. I knew it and felt the power. I hit him a few more times. He barely responded.

In the second round I cornered him against the ropes. He folded up like a beach chair and turned his back to me. I didn't want to hit him in the back. I stepped back, and the referee stopped the fight and declared a TKO. I won my first fight and got fifty bucks. I was feeling pretty confident.

The only problem was Tony's brother, Angel. Angel was angry I beat up his kid brother. He was a professional fighter and wanted to come in the ring with me. He came up to me after the fight and started poking me in the shoulder with his finger, yelling, "You think you're so tough?"

Out of no where comes my brother Vinny. "You got a problem?" Vinny had an imposing figure.

Angel, thinking he could handle Vinny, said, "Yeah, that punk beat up my kid brother."

Very coolly, Vinny said, "It was a fair fight."

Angel, still itching to punch somebody, replied, "Who the hell are you? How 'bout you and me settle the score?" Before Angel knew what was happening, Vice Grip Vin had the guy up against the wall in a choke hold.

"I suggest you play nice with my kid brother." After Vinny showed Angel the error of his ways, he was very nice to me. It was one of those proud but embarrassing moments. Proud my brother scared the shit out of him, but embarrassed that he didn't let me handle the matter. But that was Vinny, always looking out for the family.

Either way, Hornsman was thrilled at our victory, and I could see dollar signs in his eyes. But that was short-lived because brother Vinny decided after seeing me fight that he was going to manage me. And it goes without saying, you always stick with family.

My second fight was at Madison Square Garden. Vin had entered me in the professional fights. My brother told me to try a different strategy. He said to go easy on the guy and make the fight look like a struggle. After the guy knocked me for a loop, Vinny yelled, "Don't just stand there like a dumb ass. Kill the bastard." I won my next six fights.

I felt as if I was on top of the world. Making money from pool and the fights, being the tough guy in class, and bringing home straight A's. I was finally able to get my own car.

I got a two-door convertible—a miniature Model A Ford two-seater with a tiny box. It was a hardtop. My first car and I was damn proud of it. I gave all my friend rides. We'd squish in the two seats like clowns in the little car at the circus.

One day, me, my buddy Eddie Finger, and Fat Sue went for a spin. Sue was a nice enough girl, just that there was too much of her. She had a great sense of humor and was fun to hang around with. We were standing on the corner of my house just yapping away when Sue said, "Let's go get some ice cream." A typical Sue request. There was a reason she weighed one hundred and ninety nine pounds. God forbid you added on that extra pound and said two hundred, she'd belt ya one. Anyway, she made the ice cream suggestion, and Eddie and I looked at each other and said, "What the hell." So the three of us jammed into the two seats. I was driving and Eddie was wedged in between Sue and me. Actually sitting on top of her was more like it. Sue got a thrill, the closest she came to having a guy. She even tried to cop a feel.

We rode down to the ice cream joint that was a few blocks away. I debated at first letting her jog beside the car, but my gentlemanly ways would not have it.

We made it to the shop, squished but unscathed. Eddie hopped out. I got out and was waiting for Fat Sue to do the same. And we waited and waited. Then she started to make these rocking motions. What a production. Then the rocking stopped and all we heard was "Shit, I'm stuck."

"C'mon, Sue, no time to play games. Get out," I said.

"Frankie, damnit, I'm stuck in your matchbook of a car."

"Hey, watch what you say about my car. It got us here, didn't it?"

Then Eddie reached in the car. "Give me your hand."

She extended her hand. Eddie gave a tug and all we heard was, "Ouch!"

Now I started to believe her. "I'll be damned, you're really stuck. Let's get some butter and slide you out," I joked.

"Very funny, Frankie. Now get me out of your damn car."

Eddie and I looked at each other, laughed, and started to walk away. We were just kidding, of course, but Sue panicked. "Get back here!"

Eddie and I turned around. "Us?" We could be annoying when we wanted to.

So now we had to devise a strategy. "Eddie, you pull her arms, I'll go around the other side and push."

We started pulling and pushing. All the while, Sue cried, "Damn. Ouch. Watch your hands, pal."

"Hey Sue, I'm not trying to get fresh, I'm trying to get your ass out of my car. Come on, let's try again. Ready Sue? One...two..."

"Okay guys, push!" She braced herself and let out one of those blood-curdling screams. I thought Fay Wray had taken possession of her body. "Let go! You're hurting me!" Just then an Irish police officer came around the corner and heard this. He came running up to us. He grabbed Eddie by the shoulder, pulled him back, and with a real heavy brogue yelled, "Why don't you boys pick on someone you're own size?"

Boy there's a laugh; she was our size plus one.

I came running out of the car and said, "Officer, you don't understand, she's stuck."

"And the President's a leprechaun," he snorted. Then, as if on cue, Sue let out a loud wail that was somewhere between a laugh and a snort. You couldn't tell if she was laughing or crying. The police officer

53

poked his head in and said, "You okay, miss?" She started laughin' again. Tears were rolling down her cheeks.

"Miss you okay?" he repeated, causing her to crack up even further. She tried to speak, but only gasps of air got out.

"I'm...I'm..." Finally, she blurted out, "I'm stuck!"

"Well I'll be damned," the police officer replied as he scratched his curly red hair. "So you are. Where's a camera when you need it?" He looked up at us, no apology. We shrugged our shoulders. "Told ya."

"Okay boys, let's get her out." It sounded more like a command to back up a tractor-trailer. He rolled up his sleeves and started barking out orders. "You hold the door wide open," he told Eddie. Then he looked at me. "Don't just stand there. Grab something!

I grabbed her right leg. Well actually her knee.

"On the count of three. One, two, three." We all yanked, and Sue yelled "OWWW! STOP! I'm not freaking Gumby, you know."

Now this was getting serious. I liked Sue, but I sure as hell didn't want to ride around with her in my car till she lost enough weight to slide out. "Well, Officer, what do you suggest?" I asked. (Besides a diet, I thought.)

"Time for backup. I'm calling the fire department." He got on the horn and called, trying to sound serious as he described the situation. He was right, it was a Kodak moment.

By this time a small crowd had gathered outside the ice cream parlor. I was tempted to sell tickets. Then, in a typical Sue manner, while we are sitting there waiting for the fire department to come, Sue said, "Hey Frankie, the least you can do is buy me that ice cream I wanted."

"Buy you an ice cream! You're nuts. The last thing I want to do is have you wedged any farther in my car," I said.

"Frankie, you and Eddie pulled and pushed on me so damn hard that I'm black and blue. This is embarrassing enough, get me a damn ice cream."

She was right. So I bought her an ice cream. As she was eating it the fire truck pulled up sirens and all. It seemed as if the whole neighborhood was gathered around.

The fireman got out, and I swear they looked as if they were going to laugh. I mean it's not like it was an accident or something of life or death. Here is a fat broad eating an ice cream wedged in a car, and they have to get her out. I know this was one for their books.

They tried everything short of Yoga. Onlookers were screaming out ridiculous suggestions. "Pack her in ice and she'll shrink." "Get her a girdle." "Use a crane." "Call Ripley's."

Finally, they had to take the door off the hinges, and that extra few inches was the difference that managed to get her out. When she emerged from my vehicle, the crowd cheered. Never one to lose an opportunity, she raised her hands in victory and then bowed and walked away. Then she glanced back over her shoulders and with a gleam in her eye said, "Hey Frankie, don't I get a lift home?"

I sat there for a long time looking at my poor car. Sue was okay. Her ego was slightly bruised, but she made the best of it. Not to be outdone, I shook my head in disbelief, threw the bent door in the car and drove off with Eddie. I can still hear Sue's laughter as we drove by.

Yup, them were the days. I would have kept on going with my adventures and fights, but fate had other plans for me. One night after another victorious fight, I was laughing and not paying attention to where I was going. I was feeling pretty good about myself. I think I was even singing. Then next thing I knew I stepped off the curb outside the Garden. I heard screeching. Someone yelled, "Lookout!" Then a loud thump followed by excruciating pain as my legs buckled under me. I stared up at the dark sky and saw figures slowly fade together.

The next thing I knew I was in St. Vincent's Hospital in Manhattan looking at the chest of some homely nurse. I'm not sure which was worse, the damaged leg or her mug.

Later I found out that I was hit by some asshole cabby with a suspended license. The jerk broke my leg and ended my fighting career, at least in the ring, with one fell swoop.

I was really upset even though I joked on the outside. Joking was always my survival tactic. It still is. That's my way of dealing with things. Life's funny:

one second everything's going great, then BOOM, it can all change in a heartbeat. It shows us how vulnerable we all are, so we better enjoy each moment and live it to the fullest. That's what I planned to do.

This time, my brother Joey was there to pick up the pieces. He convinced me it was time to make some money...legitimately. He appealed to my sense of reason...money. He told me I could make a lot of money as a truck driver. That I could satisfy my love of cars, make Moma and Pops proud, and get everything straightened out and back on track once I got my diploma. I could see he was really concerned and serious. I loved that guy; he was watching out for his kid brother. I was going to make him proud, he'd see.

To make sure, he said he'd it set up. All I needed to do was see a guy named Louie Patooie. "Louie Patooie?" I said, "Come on Joe, what the hell kind of name is that? What is he a cartoon character?" Joey just gave me a look. "Sorry, Joey. Don't worry, I'm goin', I'm goin'. But Louie Patooie?"

I looked, he shrugged, and we both laughed.

Chapter Five

Trucking seemed like a good option. In those days, you didn't need a special classification to drive a truck under two tons. Today you need to take a special test to get a special permit. They make it so hard and expensive for a guy to make a buck.

As soon as I got out of the hospital I went down to Johnny's Bar and Grill in the Village to meet this Louie Patooie guy. I was sitting there on a slightly torn red leather bar stool eating my greasy, but delicious hamburger, when this guy shaped like the letter O tapped me on the shoulder.

"You Frankie?" he asked.

"Yeah," I said, swallowing my half-chewed meat carcass.

"Louie Patooie." He smiled and extended his well manicured hand. One gold tooth glittered in the afternoon light as he spoke. I liked the guy immediately; he reminded me of a fallen cherub. He had light brown curly hair and mischievous eyes, and he smelled like Avon soap, the kind on a rope—a smell you don't often associate with a truck driver.

"If you're finished, we can head on down to B & B Trucking and meet the boss."

"Done," I said, stuffing the last bit of hamburger in my mouth. A quick swipe with the napkin, and I threw down enough money to cover the meal and make the waitress happy for a day. I watched as Louie noted my move and silently approved of my generosity. A tacit code amongst us men. No one likes a cheapskate.

As we walked over to Hudson Street Louie told me about the other outfit he was working at. Birds of a feather travel together, and he got wind of this opening at B & B. Louie was coming with me to pave the way.

As we walked into the lot, an old cat meandered along looking like he'd seen better days. The cat was all black. Louie laughed, "There's a good sign…a black cat crossing our paths."

I laughed too. Superstition was never my thing. Louie continued, "In my book, a black cat is good luck just disguised as a bad rap." A different way of looking at it, but I liked his attitude.

As we were bullshitting about the cat, out of a rundown trailer that doubled as an office, came Charlie Lombardi.

Charlie was a gruff, lanky old man who had no time for lots of questions. "Get to the point and move on" was his attitude. Sensing this, I didn't want to mince any words. He walked over to us expectantly.

"You ever drive a truck, kid?" he asked, giving me the once over.

"Well I…"

Louie slid in. "Charlie, I'm Louie from over at Pete's Trucking. Frankie the kid…"

"…what experience do you have?" he interrupted.

63

Undaunted, Louie continued, "Experience? He's one damn good fighter. Beat the crap out of Lucky Larry...Larry ain't been so lucky since. Frankie here's had six KO's before his leg got messed up by a cabby. We're just trying to get him back on track."

Charlie grinned. "A fighter, huh? I used to fight myself. Okay, you start tomorrow at six a.m. sharp. If you're late, you're fired. "Tell your friend there to give you some lessons. Then we'll get you up to speed in no time."

"Thanks, Charlie." I offered my hand. He just turned, put up his hand in a gesture of dismissal, and walked away.

Louie and I went over to his job and practiced on his truck. That's how it was in those days, everyone helped everyone. It was like one big family if you were Italian.

Driving a truck came easy to me. In a few hours I was backing up, turning the rig around, and feeling pretty confident for the next day's work.

B & B Trucking was more of a messenger service outfit. In the morning I'd pack up a load of merchandise and bring it back to the lot. It was inventoried, then the following day it was delivered to a bunch of different stores. It paid minimal because they weren't long hauls. It lacked the adrenaline rush of a good fight and there was no glory, but it was a steady paycheck and I didn't need to take a few punches. The most I had to deal with were a few sarcastic remarks from Charlie.

After a few months of working I was getting used to the routine. Louie Patooie stopped by to see how I was getting on.

"Hey Frankie, you look good, kid. How's it going?"

"Not bad, Louie. Thanks again for all your help. If I could ever do you a favor, just let me know."

"Well I'm glad you brought that up, kid. I was thinking about you when a job offer came up. Would you like to make a little money on the side?"

"Sure. More trucking jobs?"

"Nah, a one-time deal just for a little information," he continued.

My senses started to prickle. I heard a deal coming on. Hell, there was no harm in listening. "Yeah, go ahead." So shoot me, I was curious.

"The next time you have a lightweight pickup, you know, small stuff like blenders, irons, etcetera just give me a holler and let me know."

"Just call you?" I repeated.

"Never call, kid. Stop by my house and let me know. I'll take it from there."

"What's in it for me?" I questioned.

"It'll be worth your while. Plus, you owe me one."
He winked. "Can I count on you?"

"Yeah, sure," I said. Louie walked away. So Louie was on the take. I knew my brother Joey didn't have a clue, and of course who was I to burst his bubble?

A few weeks went by and a pickup of blenders came in. I parked the truck; the blenders were inventoried and left in the lot. Even though the office was on the lot, the lot was still a rental. Other outfits also parked their trucks there. Charlie basically rented a desk and phone in the trailer, and the cat was community property. I walked straight from work to Louie's house. I knocked on the door, but Louie came outside and said, "Take a walk with me."

We walked, and I said, "Blenders, about two hundred of em."

"Which number is your truck?" Louie asked.

"License TCK24"

"Got it. Thanks kid, you'll be paid in a few days."

That was it, so simple, done? I thought. My puzzled look made him confirm. "Done," he said and then quickly walked away.

That night I knew what was going down. I figured I had better be someplace conspicuous just in case. So I went down to the pool hall.

I felt my adrenaline flowing again. I wanted to be there, to see how it was pulled off. How would he get past the guard cat? Better yet, how is he going to get to the truck in the lot? I wanted to tell someone—Vinny—or better yet, Joey. He's the one who told me to stay clean. Did he know his pal was up to a blender heist? No way. But it goes against all my ethics to squeal. Besides, at this point it was all hearsay. Ah, the masks people wear. The more you think you know them, the more you realize you only know what people want you to see of them, or of what you choose to see.

I was enjoying the trucking job, but it was pretty lifeless. If I could go back to fighting I'd get the restlessness out of my system. I needed excitement. This was the first time out of the ring I felt a tinge of adventure. Doing what you're not supposed to do always has that element of suspense, just on the verge of getting caught. Something Hitchcock could master with celluloid. But since I wasn't about to launch a film career, doing harmless jobs was the next best thing. As long as nobody was hurt, it was okay.

The next morning when I got to work, Charlie called me in to his office. I wasn't nervous, and even if I was, I'd never have shown it. Years of poker had taught me that.

"Yeah, Charlie, what's up?" I said as I strolled in.

"Your truck's gone." He just stared at me intently as if his eyes had built in laser lie detectors. I stared back.

"Where was the guard?"

Charlie relaxed a bit more. "Here. He swears he didn't see a damn thing—bastard was probably asleep as usual. I'm gonna confer with the guy who hired him and get that jerk fired. This isn't the first time it happened. Who the hell knows, maybe he's in on it."

"Wow, hard to find good help," I said, shaking my head in disbelief.

"You mocking me, Frankie? Everyone is expendable."

"No sir, just repeating something my dad always said."

"Damnit." Charlie was about to bang the desk, but he stopped himself. "Now go out there and work with Pete today on his truck. Gotta file a damn police report. Pain in my ass," he mumbled.

"Charlie..."

"What!" he said, annoyed.

"I can't work with Pete. He stinks to high heaven."

"I didn't ask you to kiss the guy, Crooks, just work with them. Now go before I charge you for your load and dock your pay for wasting my time."

I turned and walked out. That felt weird. I couldn't tell if he knew I knew and didn't care or didn't have a clue. It was insurance money but still wouldn't make his company look good. All in all, he took it in stride. He seemed more annoyed with the paperwork than the disappearance of the truck.

Two days later as I was heading home I saw Louie outside my house. He smiled and said, "Hey Frankie." As he hugged me I felt his hand slip into my coat pocket. He tapped my chest and said, "Nice job. See ya around, kid." Why do tough guys always call a younger guy, kid? Who the hell cares, I thought.

I waited for him to get out of sight. I ran into the hallway, up the stairs, and into my apartment. I was the first one home. I checked inside my pocket. There, in an envelope, was three thousand in cash. Bingo! Just like that for a little information. This was fantastic. It took me weeks to make that kind of money in trucking. I felt myself anxious to do more, but as my older brother Vin used to say, "Greediness leads to sloppiness."

That was the only job we pulled at B & B. I spent my money a little at a time so it wouldn't look suspicious. I figured I'd stay past Christmas so there was a long enough lapse before I quit. Patooie never mentioned another job again.

I had enough time to think and was debating whether I should stay straight or pull a few of these jobs here and there. Then, like a bolt of lighting, the decision was laid out for me.

On Dec. 7, 1941, Pearl Harbor was attacked. The next day the United States joined the Allied forces and entered World War II. I was a little embarrassed that the Italians were fighting against us. I was angry that the war had to call upon my brothers. Joey knew his number was coming up and volunteered to be drafted with his friends. Bum luck, they took him early and then assigned him to the Navy. Vin was drafted and very upset. He vowed to get himself dismissed.

I decided it was time to take some action of my own. Now it was just Teresa and me at home to help out Mom and Dad. The salary at B & B wasn't going to do it. I made my decision. I went over to Patooie's and told him I wanted to work with him. He nodded his head, smiled, and said, "Welcome aboard, kid."

Chapter Six

I got the job at Service International, and Louie Patooie, his friend Tony B., and I became partners in crime. We ran some card games and sold fireworks, but our plans kept getting interrupted by Uncle Sam.

I was eighteen now, and all my buddies started to get drafted. I didn't mind because we'd all be going away together. As lady luck would have it, I also met a wonderful girl, Nellie, at the same time.

Talk about a twist in cupid's fate. Nellie was dating Louie's brother Paulie at the time I met her. Paulie was a very jealous and insecure type. I hate those types because they're a pain in the ass. Any move someone makes they take it the wrong way. You gotta walk on eggshells around them or they crack. Like Joe Pesci's character in *Goodfellows*.

Insecure people remind me of little Chihuahua dogs, always yapping in their high-pitched bark at something. You blow your nose, they bark. You scratch your leg, they bark. Damn little nervous dogs. I guess, though, if I was a small, brown, ugly dog with big eyes and a disproportionate body, I'd feel insecure too. God sure does make up some funny-looking creatures.

Nellie seemed too confident for Paulie, but none the less they were dating. In those days you didn't go steady with a girl. If you liked her you dated her.

Paulie, who always hung around with Louie and me, suggested we all go on a triple date. Paulie was a weird one. He always needed approval on his girls. Like he couldn't make up his own mind. All night long he would glance over at you to see if you approved. But then if you glanced too long he'd get nervous you were hitting on his girl.

Anyway, I don't know why, but we all agreed. At the last minute Louie had to bail out. It left just the four of us; Paulie, Nellie, me and some girl whose name I can't even remember. I hate that—at the time someone is important to you, or at least is in your life, and then years later you can't even remember their name or what they look like. I don't even drink much, so I can't even blame it on that. I remember we went out, had a nice time, and that was it.

Actually, there was much more to it. I thought Nellie was a knockout—a beautiful girl with dark black hair and light skin. She reminded me of a cross between Snow White and Liz Taylor, except she had freckles. Disney's characters never have freckles, not the leading ladies anyway. Nellie was a real bombshell and very popular, but she knew it. She played it like Scarlett O'Hara in the opening scene of *Gone With the Wind*. Even though she was with Paulie, I knew I was the best guy for her, and she'd soon come to her senses and know it too. Hey, it's not that I'm conceited— some things in life you just know.

Even though we acted cool, Paulie must have sensed, or rather feared, something. After the date he came up to me.

"So what did ya think of *my* girl, Frankie?"

"She's okay. Kinda of cute." I shrugged.

"Yeah, well unfortunately she thought you were kind of a hood, and too conceited. She thought you were low class."

"Well, I didn't want to hurt your feelings, Paulie, but she's got her nose so high in the air she can smell Jupiter. And what's with those freckles? You can play connect the dots with those things."

For the next few weeks, Paulie kept fueling both Nellie and I with tales of our mutual hatred, hoping to forever lodge a wedge to keep her safe for him. His plan backfired one night when he threatened to break up with Nellie if she didn't spend Thanksgiving with his family. He told her he would take another girl and break up with her.

To which I'm told she replied, "Okay, have a good time."

Trapped by his own words and his ego, they broke up. So naturally being one to always seize an opportunity, I called her.

"Hey Nellie, this is Frankie," I said with all the charm I could muster.

"Why are you calling me?" she replied shortly.

"I heard you and Paulie split up. I thought you'd get his goat if we went out as if we were on a date. Just to rub it in." There was that deadly pause, which all men face. Is she gonna say yes or no?

"That sounds like a great idea," she answered.

"I'll pick you up at six tonight." I jumped in before she could change her mind.

"Tonight? No, sorry. You got to give me advance notice," she said half humorously. Then she added, "Eight and it's done."

"Eight it is." I grinned inside and out.

That went rather smooth.

Nellie had spunk and wouldn't take crap from any guy. To top that off, she was a virgin, and she wasn't planning on giving it up till she got married. Which was even more of a challenge. But I could handle it and give her a run for her money. She seemed to get a perverse pleasure out of giving guys a hard time. I heard Paulie was late once picking her up, so she stood him up altogether the next time. Which was quite a laugh since she was known as the Queen of Lateness.

I picked her up sharply at eight. We went to a movie and then a local ice cream place where we knew we'd either run into Paulie or word would get back to him that we were together. Despite our pretending we were just doing it for a little innocent revenge, we had a nice time and decided to see each other again. This could be a habit, I thought. A nice habit that I could grow to like.

Dating Nellie proved not to be so easy. She always made me wait a week to see her again. Once I had to cancel a date and she didn't seem to mind at all. That really got me. She wasn't like the other girls that would hang around me. They'd call me with some bogus excuse just to talk. I wasn't used to chasing after a woman, especially if I wasn't too sure how much she liked me. A man doesn't want to hang around if he's not wanted.

I'm gonna let you in on a little secret, ladies. Our egos need stroking and I break the male code of ethics to mention it. The ego is the most delicate thing about a guy. We come off all macho, as if we could shrug off the world, but we need to feel needed and want you to look up to us. That's why we never stop and ask for directions. In our minds that means we admit we don't know something. Besides, why would some stranger know how the hell to get to where I'm going?

I know it sucks, ladies, but it's the way of the world. Make a guy feel needed and you have him eating out of your hand. Make him feel useless, and you drive him crazy and crush his ego. Listen to him, act interested, and he's yours forever...that is, if you keep playing the game.

Anyway, I was starting to feel a vice grip on my ego, and I didn't like it at all. I decided to tell Nellie that it was over. I drove over to her apartment. She lived on the fourth floor of a building on McDougal Street. I caught the outer door as someone was leaving, so I didn't have to ring the bell. I walked up the flight of stairs and went to her door. I knocked.

"Who is it?" her mother's muffled voice called through the door.

"It's Frankie," I answered, as I heard the bolts being unlocked and then the door open. Two hundred locks for a door you can punch your hand through.

"Hello, is Nellie home?" I asked politely.

"No, sorry Frankie, she's out for the evening." I liked her mother, Josephine. She was a real lady and real pretty, too.

"Was she expecting you, Frankie?"

"No, I wanted to surprise her. I guess I'll call her later."

"Okay, Frankie, nice to see you. I'll tell her you stopped by." She nodded and closed the door.

I turned to walk down the stairs. I made it down one flight when I heard Nellie's voice coming up the stairs. I hid in the stairwell. Damn, there was no place to run. Okay, so big deal, she sees me here. I'll just tell her that I don't think we should see each other anymore.

As I was planning out my speech, Nellie came up the last flight of stairs with Sam Flinnegan. She was in mid sentence when saw me. Without missing a beat, and as if it was the most natural thing for me to be in her hallway, she said, "Frankie, what brings you here?"

Sam just stared at me. Sam was as Irish as they come. A big guy, six foot one with reddish brown hair, a square jaw, deep set eyes, and built. All he needed was a damn kilt and he could have been the poster boy for Celtic Airways.

I returned her coolness. "I was just in the neighborhood and wanted to say hello." I stood my ground. After all I was better-looking than this putz. Just then Sam chimed in. "Well you've said hello." Careful Sam, I thought. You're wearing your jealous ego on your sleeve.

Smooth as a Cheshire cat, Nellie said, "Sam, Frank. Frank, Sam," as she introduced us. We reluctantly shook hands and said our cursory hellos, neither knowing where the other one stood. The only one seeming to enjoy this was Nellie. She moved a few steps and like idiots we followed. "Well, boys, I'm tired. I'm going to sleep."

She had her keys poised in hand. She got to the door, turned to Sam, and said, "I had a nice time, thank you." Then she turned to me and said, "Nice seeing you again, Frankie." And before either of us knew what had happened she was inside the house. We heard the doorbolt lock. We both looked at each other dumbfounded, shrugged our shoulders, and headed down the steps. Neither of us offered information.

When we got to the main door, we both tried to head out at the same time, making it slightly embarrassing as we both got stuck in the doorway. Being the nice guy that I am, I swept my hand forward and said, "Ladies first." He gave me a look like "I outta belt you," but decided against it and left. There I stood on the stoop thinking...women! So damn frustrating...can't live with 'em. Can't live without 'em. I went home to rethink my strategy.

Chapter Seven

My strategy was to play it cool like I always did with girls. Girls always want you more if you act like you are not fawning all over them. It's psychological warfare. They want what they can't have. But you can't play it too cool otherwise they think you are totally not interested. Just enough so they want you around, but not so much that you look like a lap dog. Unfortunately, sometimes it works reverse. But the way I look at it is, there are plenty of girls out there and I'm not gonna chase after them. It drives them crazy.

I waited a few weeks before I called her again. I thought for sure she would call me, but she didn't. That was a blow to my ego. We didn't have answering machines, pagers, or cell phones back then. Today there is just no privacy—someone can catch you in the john, in your car, or on a mountaintop these days. Back then it was just the plain old phone. It rang. You answered. You talked. Boom. Simple. Unless of course you got a mother or sister on the other end. Then it depended on how reliable the person answering the phone was. This gave you the built in excuse to call again—just in case they didn't get the message. But if they did, then it was embarrassing because the person knew you were just using it for an excuse. So I assumed Nellie got the message and was being a real ball buster. Now there's a descriptive phrase and a painful one if you think about it. Exploding nuts.

We both were very stubborn. Then I thought, this is really stupid and a waste of my time. I'll just forget about her and move on to the next girl.

So one night, while I was out with this gorgeous blonde girl at the local ice cream shop—the same one Fat Sue got stuck outside of—who walks in but Nellie with some Nordic-looking blonde guy escorting her. We were both at the counter pretending not to notice each other, which was pretty hard since we were practically touching elbows. She was acting attentive to her date, me to mine. Neither one of us let on that we knew each other. Pretty childish, but most games of the heart are.

After we ordered, we both happened to look over our shoulders at the same time. We were caught. The twinkle in her eyes made me know this was foolish. I called her up and we started dating again, after mutually giving each other some shit. We got together under the pretense that we were each being generous and giving each other "just one more chance."

I was feeling pretty confident then, and my sense of humor almost blew it for me again with Nellie. One night, thinking I'm a smart guy, I told Nellie that I thought it would be nice if we could go on a double date with some friends to Scapi's bowling alley upstate. We went out and ate and on the way back from the restaurant I purposely took the darkest roads possible. As I passed a cemetery, I acted like the car was starting to stall. Then I purposely let it stop right near an open grave. Nellie was in the front seat with me, and the other couple in the back. I told Nellie I was going for help. I walked away from the car, snuck around the trees, and started walking towards the headlights with a Frankenstein mask on. Nellie was busy chatting away with the couple in the back. They spotted me first and opened their eyes wide. Nellie turned around saw me coming and screamed. In one leap she jumped over the back seat and into the lap of the couple, screaming and screaming. I laughed hysterically and finally took off the mask. I was dying. It was the funniest thing to me. I got back in the car, and she was silent. Too silent. I was still laughing. I started the car up, turned to her and said, "Come on, that was funny. Don't you think?" She turned and said, "This is what I think." and belted me in the eye with a right hook. I stopped laughing. I had a nice shiner for a week. But it was worth it. Oddly enough, it made me love her more.

So now I had my gal and I'd been called upon to serve my country. All the heroic crap that the movies make you believe. My mom, of course, was sick to her stomach that her last, and the baby, boy of the family, was going off to serve America. But a man's gotta do what a man's gotta do. Or so they say.

I showed up at the Whitehall Street Recruit Hall to get my physical. Not an impressive building for such major events to be happening inside, drafting young men to fight and further serve the cause of freedom. A noble cause, and I always love a good fight, but it is weird to think you may never come back. But we all gotta go sometime. Might as well die a hero. After all, if it was good enough from my dad, who came to America to work and wound up getting drafted after a few weeks and shipped to France for a year to fight, then it was good enough from me.

We stood on a long line, waiting for our names to be called. Everything is a damn line. A line to be called, a line to the physical, a line to fill out some forms. I hate waiting on lines. I read somewhere once that the average person spends three years of their lives waiting on line! That's 1,095 days, what a waste! Add that in with the time you spend sleeping and that's a lot of time doing nothing!

They called my name and off I trotted like a brazen stud into the little green room for a physical. The usual doctor stuff. Breathe, stick out your tongue, check your eyes, and all the holes in your body. The only part I hated was that cough. You guys know what I mean? What doctor in his right mind wants to hold another man's zeppolis in his hand? Why would you choose to do this? It amazes me sometimes the mentality that people have to have to do certain jobs. But then look who's talking. I stole baptismal certificates from a priest. It is strange how the mind will justify things and allow you to go on as if all this stuff we do as humans is normal. We humans can justify anything. Anything as long as we have what we feel is a good reason.

Beat your child, hey...he wasn't listening. Lie to your mother, hey...if I told her she would have had heart attack. Cheat on taxes, hey...the government gets enough of our money, and besides, they expect you to do it. On and on with the crap that fits our needs. The key is not to trick yourself into believing that it's true. Admit what you do, and why you do it, and you can live with yourself. To thyself be true. That Shakespeare guy had something there. At least I think it was him who said it.

So there I was with this doctor and his little clipboard checking me out like a race horse. After twenty minutes I was listed as A1. Fine specimen. I was proud.

I waited for my buddies one by one to come out of the little green cubicles with their entrance papers.

Ralphie, Paulie, and a bunch of other guys I recognized from school were all on the list. We made the cut. Eddie Finger was supposed to be there, but somehow he managed to get out of being called.

We all got notices to report for duty in two weeks. I figured since I had only two weeks left I better make them good ones. I quit my job. I mean who the hell knows what's gonna happen. Might as well live it up. Live everyday as if it's your last, and someday you'll be right.

For the next two weeks it was party time. I played card games and won money. I'm a damn good card player. Poker face, counting cards, I knew all the tricks. Nellie and I were getting along great.

One day we decided with a bunch of our friends to go swimming at the local swim club. It was a city-owned thing so you didn't have to pay. That was both the good and bad of it. It was free, but then any jerk off the street can come in and who the hell knows when the last time they showered was. I mean, there was a big sign that said, "Shower *before* you enter" but still, there were lots of bodies in there and no one was doing a shower check. Not that it really bothered me, because sometimes when I'm tired I can go a few days without a shower myself. Don't let it gross you out—men are just pigs sometimes. Here's one for you. I've even peed in the pool. Tell that to a girl and she'll go running.

Anyway, we were all swimming around and having ourselves a real good time. Playing chicken with the broads. I love that game. A girl sits on your shoulders while you're in the water. Another girl sits on her guy's shoulders and the two girls battle it out. The first one to dump the other one in, wins. None of them want to get their hair wet, so they really battle with all their might. Nellie was a pretty strong cookie, and she usually managed to dump the other girls in.

Fat Sue was there and she yelled over to me, "Hey Frankie, how about you and I teaming up?" Thank God I was with Nellie. I mean I like Fat Sue and all, but I don't need to have my shoulder bones jammed into my ankles, if you get my drift. I'd wind up looking like Wiley Coyote after he falls off a cliff, squished like an accordion. "Not today, Sue," I yelled back.

She smirked and said, "Not any day, Frankie, who you kidding. Kiss my ass."

Now there was a frightening thought! "Keep dreaming, baby," I replied. The thing is I liked Fat Sue. She was one of the guys. We both smirked at each other. That was our way. It sounded nasty, but no harm was done.

After a few hours of horsing around, we left the pool. That night my ear started to hurt. I didn't think much about it. The next day it was throbbing, so I took an aspirin and forgot about it. I had more important things to think about. My two weeks were almost up, and soon I'd be applying my street fighting knowledge on the battlefields of enemy grounds.

The Friday before we had to report in, the whole neighborhood had a going away party for me and my two pals who were leaving. Ralphie, Paulie, and I were touched. We toasted, cheered, and talked of bravado. There was a feast, with banners and presents. I felt like the freaking president or something. It was a real great time and nice to know I'd be missed by so many people.

I was thinking of asking Nellie to marry me, but I thought I should wait till I got back. No use asking a girl then getting killed or something and she's all bummed out. I mean I hoped she would be bummed out if something happened, but no need to be bummed out and tied up at the same time. My better judgment said wait.

After the party was over, it felt kind of weird. All the remnants of the party with the leftovers, crushed plates, and things laid around. Memories of a great time. Streamers and confetti all over the place. I went to sleep that night thinking how it would be to fight in a war. I pictured myself doing clever maneuvers and sitting in the trenches with the guys. I'm sure I'd find the humor in the service, it was my one surefire survival tactic.

That Monday, Paulie and Ralphie came by so we could all go together to the recruitment hall. Nellie was there also to say good-bye as I went off to boot camp.

The three of us got a lift from Eddie Finger since he wasn't enlisted. I'd really like to know who he knew that got him out of this, maybe it was a perk of knowing the wise guys or maybe it was just that weird spoon-shaped scar. Maybe some sergeant didn't want to stare at that scar all day. Maybe he knew it would make him laugh and then he couldn't keep the decorum in the room. Who knows what goes through people's minds? I do know that scar is moronic, and if

I was a girl, I don't think I'd be able to stare at that thing and think loving thoughts. He really should think about sticking a tattoo over it or something.

Anyway, Eddie was ready to give us a lift. I turned and saw my mom with tears and said, "Ah, cut that out, Mom. I'll be back sooner than you think. At least now you don't have to clean up after me." I turned to Nellie and said, "You're all right for a girl. Please take care of my mom. I'll write you and let you know what's happening. Stay out of trouble." We all hugged. I hate that mushy stuff. Just as I was about to leave my mom said, "Hey Frankie, here's a little something to take for the ride." She handed me a basket of food. Manicotti, ham and cheese sandwiches, and eclairs.

"Mom, I'm only going a few blocks."

She looked insulted. "Just take it, Frankie, take it. Share with the boys and give some to your sergeant. Get off on the right foot. They're not gonna feed you like your moma would." She patted me on the back and hugged me. I looked at Nellie and winked. She shrugged her shoulders and grinned. Mothers!

That's how Italian mothers show their love, with food. Or maybe it's their way of just shutting your mouth so you can't answer back. Either way "Manga, Manga" was all I ever heard growing up. It's amazing I didn't look like Fatty Arbuckle. I felt ridiculous carrying the humongous basket with food, but I couldn't insult my mother.

I got in the car and smiled at the guys. "Sandwich anyone?" Then we were off. We got to the draft board pretty much in silence except for Eddie Finger, who was yakking away. Sure, his life would be the same in the next hour.

We thanked him for the lift, straightened ourselves out, and walked in the doors with bags in hand. "This is it, fellas." We walked in and were told to line up. Each one of us had his own fears, but no one showed it. That wasn't the macho thing to do. We were tough guys, and it would feel good to kick someone's ass. A sergeant came over and announced, "Any one of you boys have anything happen since the physical, outside of a minor cold? Raise your hands now." I looked at Paulie and Ralphie. They shook their heads. I thought of my ear infection. I still had it, but Christ, I didn't want to make a baby of myself. Not in front of the guys anyway. You baby yourself in front of a girl so she can pamper you. In front of a guy you take an axe to your head and say, "Not so bad." Then the sergeant's voice bellowed out again. "Don't waste our time. Anything physical ailing you outside of a cold? Speak up. This is the last chance. From then on, we warned you."

Shit, what if some guy comes sneaking up on me in the battlefield and I can't hear a damn thing because of this ear infection. My hand shot up on it's own. The sergeant saw my hand out of the corner of his eye. "Yes? What are you deaf?"

"Well, sir, as a matter of fact..."

"Just get to the point, boy."

"I have an ear infection, sir." He looked at me suspiciously, probably because I didn't raise my hand on the first shot. "Go see the doctor, Crooks."

I went into the examination room. The doctor looked at me and said, "What's your excuse?" His tone implied that I was some kind of wimp trying to get out of serving my time.

"Sir, I didn't want to get examined, but I have an ear infection."

He motioned for me to sit and began examining my ears, eyes, and throat. Then he just said, "Okay."

"Okay what?" I thought. The doc wrote something down and said, "Go wait outside, on line, kid." Great, back to the waiting.

Now I thought everything was fine. I hear my name, "Crooks...thirty day extension. Go home. Report back in thirty days when the ear's cleaned up. Dismissed."

At first I was in a stupor, then I did a silent "yes!" on the inside. Paulie and Ralphie just stared at me. "You lucky dog you."

Ralphie whispered, "Is it bull or what, man?"

"No, hey...come on, you know I had it when I went swimming at the club." Then I winked at them just to confuse them. I loved doing that. Trying to put one over on people. Especially when it is true—then you do something like wink and they think you're lying all the while you're telling the truth. Then you try to convince them you are telling the truth. The more you try, the more they don't believe you, the more you laugh at how ridiculous it is. I waved good-bye, and as I left, Paulie yelled, "Hey, Frankie. How about leaving us with the sandwiches?"

I smiled and put the basket down at their feet. "Enjoy Red Riding Hood and watch out for the wolves." I walked out. The guys didn't know what to make of my getting an extension and neither did I. But I sure as hell wasn't going to frown on good luck.

When I got back home my mom and dad were at work. Teresa was at school. Only good Ole Butch and I were there in the apartment to hangout. I love dogs, man, they are so loyal. Butch used to lick my feet. Now that is loyalty. Especially with my feet. They smell like feta cheese on a hot summer day. I sat there content, being pampered by man's best friend.

I couldn't call Nellie because she was working too. So I just enjoyed being back in my own bed for a while.

When my parents came home my mother was thrilled. "Frankie, my little boy, what are you doing here?"

My dad was a bit more skeptical. "What? Did you get thrown out again? You're not even in a day, and they throw you out. What a disgrace."

"I didn't get thrown out, Dad. I was dismissed for another thirty days till my ears clear up." I smiled. Well, that smile must have set him off because he almost totally lost his accent and started getting all excited and screaming.

"Ears clear up! You hear me fine! What kinda bullshit is this? Don't go trying to weasel your way out of being drafted. I worka my ass off every day at that dye factory. You could put a little sweat into things, Frankie. Your brother Joey, now he's a boy to make your papa proud. Not only did he go in, but he went in early to be with his friends. This is a good country. You fight for her."

I was hurt—of course I'd fight for my country. I couldn't even say anything. The lecture was over. He moved into the living room into his favorite chair.

The favorite chair seems to be a guy thing. A ritual of sorts that I think must have started with cavemen. They probably had a favorite rock to lean on, and no one would go near another man's rock. Today it's the Captain Kirk home shopping version chair. The Grand Poobah sits his butt in that chair and from there all is commanded. Of course, in my day they had no remote controls—well they did, but they were called "kids." "Hey Frankie, change the channel. Teresa, fix the antenna." We dutifully ran and did it. It was in a weird way a privilege to be the chosen one to change the antenna, that is until you are the only one left in the house, then it's downright annoying.

So Dad lounged while Mom cooked up some Rigatoni Pommodori, a poverty dish that tastes delicious and is one of my favorites for dinner. Life sank back to normal. It was as if I'd never went to enlist.

I called Nellie and she sounded pleasantly surprised and excited. It really would have stunk if she would have sounded disappointed and annoyed: "Oh it's you!" That would not have been a good sign. Men need the fanfare, the dancing woman, the special effects.

We made plans to go out after dinner, as I didn't want to wind up with a spoon scar like Eddie for not appreciating Mama's efforts. Then I decided to call Louie Patooie and told him of my good fortune. Louie was thrilled to have his partner back, at least for thirty days.

The next day, Louie and I went back to business: gambling, card games, and selling illegal fireworks. Yup, business as usual, and with my two brothers temporarily out of the way, I had no angels on my shoulders telling me which way to go. All I knew was I was making lots of money and it was easy. So I kept myself busy, taking Nellie out, making money, and enjoying my time.

Thirty days came to an end quickly. I was ready to go once again and serve my country. This time there was another farewell party, but only for me, the other guys having already left. It felt weird, but nice to be so loved and the center of attention. Again with the hugs and kisses and food and presents. This could be some racket.

The next morning, good old Spoonface did me a favor again and drove me to the center. Again Nellie was there, Moma was crying, and a basketfull of goodies was waiting. This felt more solemn, though. Maybe because it was just me and Eddie in the car. I had a feeling this was it. That sinking do or die, pit-in-your-stomach feeling.

Nellie gave me a nice note telling me to take care and all. Woman's stuff we pretend to hate but really love, as long as they don't expect us to do the same thing. She said she had thought of it last time, but forgot to do it. That's the great thing about second chances, you can make up for the things you forgot the first time around and wished you had done.

I walked into the hall and the sergeant reacted as if he knew me. "Get in line. You're the one with the ear problems, right?"

"Yes, sir, but it's all cleared up," I said proudly, ready to get this whole enlistment thing out of the way and move onto phase two.

"Good. Go get your okay from the doctor."

I walked in with my note. I felt like a second grader. The doctor took the note from me and started examining my ears. Since this was routine, I started daydreaming. I don't even remember what I was thinking, but I was a million miles away. Well, good old Doc must have asked me something. Finally, he yelled, "Hey Crooks, do you hear me? Answer!" I jumped. He jumped.

"I'm sorry, Doc. I couldn't hear you." He gave me a queer look, not in gay way or anything, just a weird look like, "Don't play me for a fool, son."

So I said, "Honest, I didn't hear you." Of course I hadn't. I was daydreaming about some girl or whatever I was thinking about. Then he scribbled something on a piece of paper, and said, "Well, your ear is still a bit infected. Thirty more days, Crooks."

I couldn't believe this. I wasn't even trying. Maybe God had other plans for me. Once again, I trudged back to my old homestead. I was feeling rejected in a one way, but happy in another. Feelings aren't always easy to pin down, especially for a street guy. Feelings were for sissies. I had them, just didn't feel the need to analyze them.

When I walked into the apartment, Butch was there ready to lick my feet. Or at least that's how I interpreted it. This time when I heard my mom coming in the door, I hid behind it and jumped out when she entered. After she jumped five feet in the air, she belted me with her bag across the left cheek. "You sonofabitch! You're gonna give your moma a heart attack." She kept hitting me with her hands. I covered my face and said "Ma, Ma, stop! I'd feel sorry for any burglar that runs into you."

Then she just stopped dead in her tracks. "What are you doing home?"

"Nice greeting, Ma. They said my ear is still swollen, so I get another thirty days."

"You better leave the house for a while till I tell your papa. He's going to think you're doing some kind of dirty business to get out of helping your country." I checked a mirror as I left the house. Thank God I didn't have a pocketbook scar on my face.

I went straight over to Louie Patooie's, but he wasn't there. I was walking by Wooster Street when this guy yelled, "Hey, kid. Need a job?" Just like that. I looked around, saw he was talking to me, and asked, "What kind of job?"

"A government job making decent money." He put his arm around me and led me inside this building. Felt like a setup out of a movie, but it was legit. This was a great time to be working. Young men were scarce, and woman were starting to be a more important part of the work force. The government needed all the help it could get from its citizens.

So I got this gravy job for this company on Wooster Street. This company got government contracts to build tripods and machinery, but didn't know where to get the labor. This guy paid me ten dollars per person, per day, to get recruits to come in and work. I went to the schools and got kids to work from three to seven. They made money, and so did I, as long as they kept coming to work.

I was set. In the days I worked with Louie making about one thousand dollars a week, and I would get recruits in the afternoon to help the government. I made a nice bundle.

When the thirty days was up I didn't want to go. I was slightly embarrassed because I knew they were having another party for me. Less people this time. It's weird that they felt obligated to throw a party in case something happened to me. They would have felt guilty if they didn't send me off with love and fanfare. So it was as much for them as it was for me.

By now leaving was a routine with me, my mom, Nellie, and Eddie. This time I didn't get a basket of food, only a few sandwiches. Nellie gave a wave and said, "See ya in an hour." We all laughed.

One hour later, I was back at my home with a final note...REJECT. Man that hurt. But it wasn't for a lack of trying. I gave it my best shot. When my mom came home that evening all she said was, "Oh it's you again. Take the garbage out."

And that was my welcome back into the real world.

Chapter Eight

My real world now consisted of easy ways to make money. With both Vinny and Joey still serving our nation, I seemed to have a tendency towards easy street, which always seemed to be the shadier side of life, but it came easy. Sudden pangs of guilt, the way a gas attack comes on and gets you in the gut, would force me to intermingle crime with legitimate stuff. It eased the pressure.

Louie Patooie and I, the dynamic duo, joined forces once again and now were shylarking, bookmaking, and doing swag as well as running illegal cards games and selling fireworks. Petty stuff really in the world of crime. For those novices, here's my little dictionary of the things we did. Bear in mind English ain't my best subject, but here goes.

Frankie's Abridged Dictionary of Relevant Terms

Definition of shylarking: When you loan money at an exorbitant rate of interest. At a rate of five for six. For example, someone borrows five dollars. If they don't give you six dollars at the end of the week they have to give you one dollar. But then they still owe you the five bucks. Until they pay the amount in full they have to give you twenty percent a week of the total borrowed.

This goes on until he pays you. Some people paid for two years at one dollar a week. If they don't pay the one dollar you threaten them—no exceptions. You explain to them that they cannot beat you, or everyone else will think they can do it, too, so they have to pay. Then you give them an example to bring the point home. "If you don't pay your electric bill, they turn off your lights, and if you don't pay us, we'll permanently turn off your lights." It's corny but dramatic. Usually people get the message and there are no problems.

Who do you lend money to? These loans are to people who you know where they live. Usually they're gamblers. They lose a hundred bucks in a card game. They want to stay in the game because gamblers always feel they can win it back. Human weakness makes them willing to borrow at this rate. We cash in on the weakness and insure with fear.

Bookmaking: Again this is dealing with people you know. There is no threat if you can't find them and collect. It's usually the same people you loan money to. With bookmaking, a person bets on sports or horse racing.

For example, a person likes the Jets. You give them a phone number to call up. Then that number transfers them to another extension automatically (like today's call forwarding...except it's done in private...you hook up your own lines). They call up one apartment and then you have a line going up to another apartment that you put in yourself—obviously the phone company doesn't know about this, and hopefully, neither do the police. You set up the phone lines and work out of the same apartment or building. If the law gets wind of this they will come to the address that the number is listed with, but you're in another apartment or location. You also have a lookout guy.

It's set up so that if someone enters the "real" apartment you know someone is in there and you shut down operations. You leave before the wire is traced to the second location. Of course, this worked back then; in today's technology this might not be so easy.

Swag: You're buying and selling stolen merchandise at a reduced rate. Blenders are swag. Every type of product is game. This is all done through word of mouth. The guys you see selling watches and stereos at crazy prices are peddling you hot merchandise. We were ahead of our time—now they have discount stores. The stolen merchandise comes off the sweat of other countries' backs. It's called kid labor. Some things oughtta be a crime, but they're not because the government is involved, and then it's called politics.

Fireworks: I don't have to explain what fireworks are but this is how we sold 'em. Louie Patooie and I were buying fireworks from a guy in New Jersey that used to do the display for the Macy's fireworks. Since we had a truck, we would bring them in and get around it. Fireworks were legal in Connecticut and North Carolina, so we would request that they would ship by our company.

A typical operation would run like this: Point A was where the order was coming from. Point C was a legal drop off, a state where fireworks were allowed.

Point B, in the middle, was New York. We would drop off fireworks in New York, and never deliver them to our Point C destination. If we got caught in transit we'd show the receipt that it was going to the legal Point C. We would resell them in New York. Whatever we didn't sell we would use ourselves.

So these are the kinds of things Louie Patooie and I were involved with. It paid the bills, fed our egos, and made for a fun night. I was feeling pretty good about myself, so I decided it was time to get serious with Nellie. But I needed cash. I knew the opportunity would present itself, 'cause it always did.

Two nights later, I was walking down Sullivan Street and found a crap game in progress being played against the side of a building. I entered the game. Anybody could get into it, as long as he had the money to make the bet. I'd bet win or lose. I'd cover the bet of the shooter. I picked up the dice and the dice rules, if you hit a seven or against the number. I watched the game, and I'd seen that the dice were running exceptionally good, what I mean is, I got on a big roll, and I was covering all bets, so within fifteen minutes I had all the money in the game. I won three thousand bucks. Before I had the temptation to spend it, I went to Jack's Jewelry Shop. I know it sounds more like the name of a pawn shop, but it was a real swanky place. I laid the entire stack of money down and bought a one-karat round diamond platinum ring for Nellie. I couldn't wait to see the expression on her face.

I called her that night. We went out to Chinatown, to a restaurant that we had frequented in that part of town. The guys there knew me because I was a big tipper. I also think they thought I was in the Mafia, so they treated me special.

I arranged for them to put the ring into a fortune cookie. I really had to trust these guys not to switch the ring. The dinner went fine. We talked about all the things that were going on. Then the cookies came out.

The waiter nearly spoiled the surprise. He was taking these tiny baby steps, one at a time, holding the plate out in front at him and just staring at it, you would have thought the damn ring was made of glass. It was kind of funny when I look back on it.

Then he set the plate with the cookies down right in front of Nellie. Nellie and I looked at each other. I just shrugged.

So then he just kept standing there with this big stupid grin on his face. I said, "Thanks Charlie" to try to give him a hint to leave. He continued to stand there, pushing the plate towards Nellie and smiling. She gave me a funny look like, "What's up with him?" I wanted the waiter to get lost. This was a special moment. Finally a ten spot gave him the hint.

I grabbed the empty fortune cookie to make sure there was no mess-up. I looked at Nellie and tried to joke it off, "Crazy Guy." Nellie smiled and took the remaining cookie. But instead of breaking it like she

119

usually did, she bit into it. She nearly broke her tooth on the ring. "Owww!" She looked down. She looked shocked and happy at the same time. Then she smiled coyly. "Are you trying to tell me something?"

"Thank God you didn't swallow the ring. We would have had to have Charlie there smack you on the back. That would've killed the romance. Well, what do you think? Will you marry me?" I said in my best Frank Sinatra macho impression voice.

She smiled, pretended she was thinking about it, then nodded "yes."

I slipped the ring on her finger and all the waiters started to clap. Everyone had been watching. It felt like a scene out of a Bogart movie. It felt good. Life was grand.

Chapter Nine

Now that I was engaged, I started to feel I needed to do something to make everyone proud of me. I was feeling a little like I'd pulled a fast one on Uncle Sam so I decided to join the National Guard on Fourteenth Street. You had to put in only a few hours a week, and nothing much every really happened. I had to train and do military exercises, but most of the time I'd sit around and play cards or gamble.

Okay, if the truth be known, it wasn't so much my guilt kicking in, but my greed for the green. You see those guys over at the National Guard were amateurs. They didn't know how to play craps and I did. I'd heard about the odds in there, even money. I just couldn't pass up an opportunity like that. I joined to get in on the games.

It went like this. In a regular craps game, every number has different odds. The numbers four and ten for example are supposed to get two to one odds. That's the way they do it in Vegas. If I bet one dollar and win, I was supposed to get two dollars back, and I wind up with three dollars back in my pocket. The numbers nine and five had three to two odds. For each two-dollar bet, you got three dollars back. You'd wind up with five dollars. A six and eight were supposed to get six to five. For every five dollar bet, you'd get six dollars back.

But that's not how they did it at the Guard. They were playing that no matter what number they'd bet, they would get the same money back. If they bet one dollar and won, they'd get one dollar back, and wind up with a total of two dollars.

Since I knew the odds and they didn't, I had a fifty percent advantage over them. I would place side bets. When a guy bet on a number that I knew was a bad bet, I would bet against him. Then I would win. It was purely mathematical.

The other racket that I had going, was I would be in their boxing show. Each National Guard outfit had some boxers. We'd have matches against each other. I would spend my time training, and they didn't care. That way I didn't have to do the mundane things like clean the tents, etc. The boxing and gambling gave me extra privileges.

It was around this time that brother Vinny went AWOL. Vinny was on a ship doing cooking duty. He had an argument with one of the other cooks and punched him. Then he was sent to the ship's psychiatrist, and Vinny told the doc to put it where the sun don't shine. At the next docking area he jumped ship and managed to find his way home.

Vinny knew he was in trouble, so he stayed home and hid for a while. We always covered for him. An unspoken Italian tradition is you stick by family right or wrong. No matter what. So, military men would come knocking on our door and we'd always say we

123

hadn't seen him. The weird thing was that my dad never questioned him, even after that speech he gave me on fighting for my country. I think parents expect different things from each of their kids. It seemed a little unfair, but I wasn't going to ask. Some things are better left unsaid.

Eventually the military caught up with him. Lots of long drawnout hearings were held. He was dishonorably discharged as a troublemaker, conceited, and not a team player, which is dangerous in time of war.

Vinny wasn't proud, but happy. He said the way he saw it, "Eagles may soar, but moles don't get sucked into jet engines." He couldn't have cared less what they thought as long as he got his way. I knew Vinny was a team player, just not on that team.

Joey was the only one, outside of Papa, who really did the family proud in the military. We got word that he'd earned some medals.

Sister Teresa had in the meantime met a nice man, married him, and moved to Florida.

I don't know what it is, but when your family starts to separate and spreads their wings to go on with their own lives, you feel this pang of guilt as if you are abandoning the people who devoted their lives to raising you. You have to balance it. I don't have that knack yet.

Then, my dad had a stroke. The doctor told him, no more working at the dye shop. He needed to relax. But my dad wanted to keep working, said that retirement would kill him. He had to find something to make him feel useful, but calm. For whatever reason my dad had a yearning to sell peanuts in Washington Square Park. So he did.

Now, my dad was a very frugal man. He refused to buy lunch outside the house, so everyday my mom would make him lunch. Being the youngest, I was elected to bring it to him.

At the time I was impressed with myself, considered myself almost a wise guy. I was a little embarrassed to have to go to the park. There is this unwritten rule, a kind of ingrained respect, that made it so I could never say "No" to my mother. That's the weird thing—all us tough guys, whether in the military or mob, knew the ultimate Capo di tutti was your mom.

It wasn't so much bringing him the lunch that bothered me, but more that I had to relieve him at the stand so he could go to the bathroom. There I was, with my gray Cadillac on the street, with the engine running, standing behind the peanut stand in a pinstriped suit selling peanuts. I prayed none of my friends would pass by. I almost tried to make it look as if I was just hanging out, not actually working the stand. This used to annoy my dad, who was on to me. He would purposely stay longer in the bathroom. He was amused at my squirming. He said, "Never be embarrassed of an honest living." But it didn't matter, I still was. I felt selling peanuts was beneath us. Not that gambling or bookmaking was better, or even that we were rich or anything. It's just that I wish it wasn't something so...ordinary.

A couple of times I thought about not going to meet my dad, but since my brother Vinny was back, he threatened he would beat me up if I didn't. Then, of course, if Teresa found out, she would slap me once or twice when she saw me. It was easier to be embarrassed than constantly get smacked on the back of the head. It's amazing I didn't develop a tumor. That was a big thing with us Italians, a whack on the back of the head. I'm sure it must have jarred something loose. It's probably the reason I think the way I do.

So one day I stood there behind the peanut stand for what seemed like longer than O.J. Simpson's trial until Dad finally strolled back from the john. I escaped my embarrassment by running to my car. I was about to pull away when I saw some drunk guy walking up to the peanut stand. He started talking to my dad. I decided to watch to make sure there was no trouble. I got out of my car so I was within ear range and could hear the conversation.

In his drunken stupor the guy said to my dad, "Hey, how come the peanuts whistle?"

My dad in his broken English replied, "Wella, you see there is this steam a-coming through the peanuts, and the air she rushes up past the peanuts and makes the whistle sound."

The drunk, totally oblivious, asked again, "But, how come the peanuts whistle?" My dad patiently, which is a rare thing for him, tired to explain again. "I tolda you, it's a the steam, she make 'em whistle."

The drunk guy asked a third time. This time my dad got so mad he yelled, "Hey mister, if a your nuts were a-roasting, you'd whistle too! Now getta the hell out of here." The guy stumbled away with one hand covering his nuts.

I laughed out loud for a long time with that one.

Chapter Ten

Things went on like that for a while. They say the only thing in life you can be certain of is change. Joey came out of the service decorated, became a cop, got married, and moved to Hester Street.

Vinny got married, too, moved to Brooklyn, and was a shylark.

I got married to Nellie. We had what they call a football wedding. None of the fancy stuff like the kids have today, spending enough money to buy a small country. A football wedding is just like it sounds: They make sandwiches and put them on a platter in the center of each table with a bottle of wine. If you have a sandwich at your table and want to switch it with a sandwich at another table you yell out, "Hey Joey, what'd you got? Wanna trade?" Then you throw the sandwich, football style, clear across the room. A ham and cheese hero flies across the room, and hopefully the receiver catches it. It's down-to-earth, good food and a lot of fun. And, you don't have to sell your first born to pay for it.

We honeymooned in Florida. I never did get to relieve Nellie of her virgin status while we were dating (don't ask) so this was a big week for us. I'm not going to give you all the details, because first, it was my wife, and second, I'm not the kiss and tell kinda of guy.

The funniest thing that happened there was when we were in the Everglades. I had Nellie jump the fence at the Al's Alligator Farm. I told her to lift the tail of the alligator so I could take a picture. She did, and at that very moment, the thing turned around and tried to bite her. She cleared the fence better than any Olympic jumper I've ever seen. I laughed so hard tears came down my face, even though Nellie was smacking me on the head. What the hell compelled me to ask my new bride to go into an alligator pit, and what made her do it, only fools in love know.

Let me tell you, though, I was not the only one with a sick sense of humor. Nellie had me take a picture or her lying in front of a car like she was dead. She sent the photo to her mother and wrote, "The honeymoon didn't turn out like we planned." Luckily we arrived home before the photo, or her mother, Josephine, would have had a heart attack.

We moved into Mario Gendarmo's old apartment on Thompson Street. It was in the same building her mom lived in. Mario told the landlord not to rent it to anybody but me. Even though I was never "made," meaning I wasn't officially in the mob, I knew the guys. It was like I freelanced with them, got paid on a per job basis, not a percentage of the whole.

It was the nicest apartment in the building, with lots of marble, real marble from Italy. Gendarmo was taking up residence for a while in a state penitentiary for tax evasion and embezzlement. The funny thing was Gendarmo's brother was our local parish priest. But no matter how much he prayed, he couldn't keep his brother out of jail. I guess every family has its extremes.

I wonder sometimes how much of our lives are influenced by our upbringing and how much by hereditary. Is it in our genes to be good or bad? Or do people just get handed a lot in life that makes them turn a certain way? There is evidence on both sides to prove that none of it matters. You can have rotten parents and turn out okay, or have great parents and still be a murderer. It's kind of scary. It's almost a crap shoot.

Now that I was married, I figured once again it was time to go straight. I opened a combination coffee shop and restaurant called "Manga Mama's" next to Louie Patooie's truck company. He had had his own company for a while now and was rolling in the dough.

133

He gave me a hand, sort of as a wedding present and became part owner of our restaurant.

It was a family-run operation, with homemade specialties. I had my mom cooking some great Italian food. Now Moma, she didn't understand the first thing about saving money in the restaurant business. When it came to food, "only the best" was her motto. She would shop for the food for the restaurant as if she were cooking for a large family. We kept telling her to shop at wholesale places, but she kept going to the corner shops and paying top price. She didn't get the economics of it all.

Honestly, I did the same thing myself a couple of times out of laziness. Nellie used to get so mad. She was a typical woman. I know I am going to be called a male chauvinist pig for that statement, but she really loved to shop for bargains. Men just don't give a shit about that. Whatever's convenient is what we go for. Okay, maybe there are a few guys who care, but really who the hell has time to go from place to place? The money you spend in gas looking for the bargain, you could've used on the extra few cents you paid. However, if we're talkin' negotiating a business deal, that's a whole other story.

Anyway, we all worked the place. Nellie's friend, Tommy Lampern, this big three hundred pound sweetheart of a guy, and my mom cooked. Rudy, Nellie's younger brother, and me served the customers. We kept my mom away from the customers because she would talk to them and start to tell them how she prepared the food. Didn't matter what they were eating, she would go on and on. No one wanted to be rude, but a guy coming in for a cup of coffee doesn't need to know the recipe to Tortellini Alfredo.

Nellie would help serve after she got out of her day job. She had a job in the photography room of this pattern place over in the garment district. She had really great ideas and loved to draw and design the clothes. The only problem was that they would change her designs so much, they never looked like what she'd originally intended. She was frustrated but loved the fashion world anyway. That's the way it works a lot of times, the workers come up with the ideas, and the company steals them, all under the name of "being a company person." Either way, she had a knack for it.

Anyway, "Manga Mama's" was a lot of fun. We had our steady stream of truckers from next door as our clientele. They ate a lot and loved our food. You know, I think it helped that we had a fat cook. That shows that the food is good. He enjoys his own food so much he can't stop. If it's some skinny little twerp cooking, then people get suspicious. You just can't be Italian, a cook, and skinny in a restaurant, because it doesn't look good. At least, that was the mentality back then. Today everybody's so damn worried about fat free, low calorie stuff. You know, my theory is that all those people are skinny because the food is so damn lousy. If you'd munch on carrots and celery all day, you'd lose weight too. But Italian food is rich, creamy, and has lots of cheese. You aren't hungry after you eat a good Italian meal. Carbo overload. Plus who the hell cares? We're all gonna die someday. I might as well enjoy the food while I'm here. I'm just glad the truckers had the same mentality as me or we'd have been out of business.

Our restaurant had its own personality. Each of us was a character. It was like we were on a set for a sitcom. The kitchen was so small that every time someone needed to get in or out of the kitchen, Tommy would have to leave the kitchen entirely, just to let them pass. There was no way around. This really pissed him off if he was in the middle of mixing something. He'd be standing outside the kitchen with his hands full of dough or dripping of sauce. Sometimes, if he got mad, which took a lot, he'd wipe it on you as you went by and you'd have this big white dough mark on the back of your shirt or butt and not even know it.

It was a restaurant with an attitude. We'd only served people we liked. If we didn't like your attitude, we wouldn't serve you. It was our place. If you didn't like it you could get the hell out. But the food was so good, people kept coming back. It was almost like they thought our carefree attitude was part of the act. Some of them seemed to like the abuse. I mean, it wasn't really like we abused them, we just wouldn't take any crap. Some stuck-up jerk snapping his fingers like he's Gods gift to creation could go take a hike. With this attitude, it makes sense that eighty-five percent of our customers were the truckers. Men with tough hides.

I remember one time this sissy-looking guy, tight upper lip type, in a business suit came in. He sat down all proper and started to inspect the forks and knives. I watched this jerk. He held a fork up to the light, rubbing it with his napkin. Really pissed me off. He did this to every item on the table. Making those "tsk tsk" sounds as he did it. Huffing and puffing like a fat man in a potato sack race.

Even though our restaurant was for truckers, a loud bunch, our place was spotless. My moma worked real hard on keeping it clean. This guy checking us out was an insult. Personally I couldn't care less—I've been known to use a cloth napkin as a handkerchief—but for the sake of my moma and Nellie, this was an insult. Sometimes you get annoyed at things because you know it will bother those you love.

After about ten minutes of annoying inspection, this guy snapped his manicured little fingers, "You. Busboy." That's all Rudy needed to hear. Rudy kept cleaning the table next to the jerk as if he didn't hear him. Then tight ass does it again. "Excuse me, busboy. I am addressing you." Rudy turned around and said, "Yeah, I heard you," and continued to clean. By now all of us were watching this interaction. A couple of my trucker friends were there, ready and waiting.

The man got up, tapped Rudy on the shoulder, and said, "I am going to complain to the manager about your behavior." Rudy smirked and said, "My behavior. MY BEHAVIOR! You're the one acting like a fool."

With that, the guy said, "Young man, do you know who I am?"

Rudy shrugged. "I really don't give a damn."

The man was beside himself, "Well! I never. You will be sorry for this rude behavior. Now, I insist you serve me."

Rudy said, "Really? Okay, I'll serve you, sir." He turned around, and as he spun back he yelled, "Water?" and splashed it on his face. At that moment, one of the truckers yelled "Food fight!" They looked at me, I nodded it was okay, and then food was flung everywhere. But mainly in the vicinity of the man. The man grabbed his coat, ducked flying spaghetti, and yelled, "You'll all be sorry," and then stamped out. We all high-fived each other and the guys helped me clean up.

The next day we had a temporary closure notice put up. Turns out he was a health inspector with no sense of humor. He closed us down for unsanitary conditions. To make matters worse, his brother was a restaurant critic and gave us a bad review in the paper. "While Manga Mama's is rumored to have excellent food, this food critic knows from a reliable source that it has horrible service. If the uncouth waiters don't like you, tempers fly, as does the food. Anyone who wants a normal dining experience, and would rather have food in their mouth instead of on their head, is strongly urged to stay away from this hellhole." His review had people flocking to us out of curiosity. They wanted to see if they could annoy the waiters and get in on the action. Business was booming for a while and we actually had to stage food fights not to disappoint our customers and live up to our press. God Bless America!

But after a while the cleanup became a pain in the ass. I had thought about giving the customers plastic food to throw at each other but it didn't have the same effect. Plus we started having frequent visits from four-legged friends. So we had to stop.

In general, restaurant business was a pain, though. Ask any restaurant owner. The hours are long and murderous. This going straight was going to kill me. The money rolls in slowly, meal by meal. I really don't mind working hard, I just like to see the rewards faster. Besides, it's miserable working with the public. Although we really didn't work "with the public." But that was part of the charm of our place. There was a restaurant in Brooklyn many, many years after our place called the Crazy Country Club, and their motto was "warm beer and lousy food." They made a mint. It's all in the timing.

Luckily, on the side, Louie and I still ran card games out of the back of the restaurant. We were the only two that knew. There was a separate back alley door that lead to the basement. Behind the storage room was a spare room. I furnished it up nice, even had its own refrigerator stocked for the guys.

That's how I kept financing "Manga Mama's." We were getting tired of the restaurant business. It was time to try another venture. Besides, Nellie was pregnant now, and I didn't want her or me to be working all kinds of crazy hours. I had to think of a better way. My mind was racing, and then I ran into Ron Casulli and Isen Brookville.

Chapter Eleven

Louie Patooie and I were still shylarking. This guy we knew, Ron Casulli, from a neighborhood men's clothing store, "Casual Wears," used to have his alterations done by this tailor, Isen Brookville. Isen, it turned out, owed us money that he had borrowed from us through a third party. The third party skipped town, and Isen still owed us the bucks.

We approached Isen about our money and we let him talk us into opening up an alterations business where he would work off his debt. I say we let him talk us into, because usually we'd just get our money, but we were looking for something else, so this seemed as good an alternative as any. Louie and I elaborated a little on Isen's plan. We figured more money could be made if we opened a combination clothes and alterations store. This way people could buy the clothes and have them fitted in the same place. A one-stop shopping deal.

I didn't trust this Isen guy with money because he was broke, but I liked his idea. I approached Ron Casulli, and the two of us went into business together. Louie kept the trucking company since he had recently gotten married he didn't want to extend himself financially any further at the moment.

Nellie was excited about the idea because it had to do with clothes, and she liked the idea of being able to decorate the store. We came up with the name "Adam and Eve." It took us a couple of months to find a place. The deal was, I put up the money and Ron's clothing expertise was his investment. He knew where to get the clothes, how to mark the latest fashions, and all the ins and outs of the business. Nellie had a fix on what was hot, too, and Isen knew how to make you look hot with his fixing. This was the first time I was really excited about a legitimate business. I was learning something new. I had an experienced partner, my wife knew the ropes, and I'd have a store my parents could be proud of on Sixth Avenue in Greenwich Village.

The store looked great. It was designed like the Garden of Eden, with two barrels of apples on each side as customers walked in. Leaves were hanging from artificial tree branches, and a big funny-looking snake was poised by the register. It had a real nice feel to it and was way before its time with theme stores like Hard Rock, Motown Café, and the The Rainforest Café.

The day we opened Nellie went into labor. Man, talk about timing.

Two of the biggest events in my life happened on the same day: July 27.

The store made $523.27 the first day, and Nellie made me a proud father of a seven-pound, seven-ounce baby girl. We named her Frances, closest thing to Frankie I could come up with for a girl. I thought it would be a boy. None the less, I swore I'd still teach her how to box, ride motorcycles, and do all the things a boy can do. But she was my beautiful baby girl. I was now on top of the world.

Adam and Eve started out as one store. In a year's time it grew into a big shop—I mean big. The rent was twelve hundred at the time, which was a lot in the early sixties. Business was good, but we wanted to make it better. So we came up with an idea.

The idea was having all the Village crafts under one roof. We had little sections of the store that we rented out to different people. They would each purchase their own merchandise, but we would keep track of it. We wanted to be diverse in our offerings, so we had a bookshop, women's accessories, leather articles, paintings, and so on and so forth.

One of the tenants was Nancy Walker. Nancy was the owner of the "Little Woman's Shop." She was a fine-looking lady, thirty-three, had a good business head, but always had a sob story. She really made you feel bad for her. The type of lady that a cop lets out of a speeding ticket.

One day, she asked Ron if we could extend her credit just for the Christmas season. She anticipated a lot of sales but just didn't have the money up front to buy the merchandise. She showed us a really fancy-looking business projection sheet. It seemed to make sense. Since the men's shop, Adam and Eve, had great credit we obliged and extended credit to her by purchasing her merchandise. Just to hold her over. She agreed to pay us back in installments.

We were able to keep track of sales since we had a central cash register, even though she physically took the money. The merchandise was labeled by department, so at the end of the day we could look at the labels and know how much each department had made.

For example, if a customer bought something it had a letter on it like B. Based on the letter we knew it came from the Bookstore section. C for Candleshop, you get the idea. We wanted to keep it simple. Nancy was true to her word; she sold a quarter of a million dollars worth of merchandise before Christmas. The scam was, she paid no bills. She showed us checks that indicated she was paying the purchase bills that we paid for, but she never mailed the checks. We thought she was keeping our credit good, but she was pocketing the money that her store was making. All profit, no liability.

After Christmas, in one season, she killed our business with a smile. Nancy disappeared and we were left holding the bills for her clothes. We had all the bills, and she had all the profits. We had been scammed into the ground. We had extended ourselves too far, and we were deep in a hole. We went belly up. Eve, disguised as Nancy, had committed another mortal sin, and me playing the part of Adam, fell once again into the trickster's trap. I guess I should have paid more attention to that lesson in church when I was an altar boy. So two and a half years of hard work vanished in the night. We were left holding our sides where there once used to be a rib.

Chapter Twelve

When in doubt go back to what you know, and for me it was crime. It's a lot less headaches. I had to make a living for my family, and I just was no good at the legitimate business. I tried it many times, and many times I failed. My ideas and schemes always seemed to work better on the shady side.

I don't know why that is. It seems if you can think of schemes to get by on the wise guy side, you should be able to apply it in the legitimate world. I think the key is though, knowing your playmates.

For some reason my senses would take leave on the straight side. When I was working with gangsters, I knew I had to watch my back because I didn't know who to trust, except for a few close friends. In legitimate business, I blindly thought everyone was on the up and up. So like a fool, I trusted them. My street smarts would go out the window if someone used bigger words than me. I was intimidated if they had more education. I allowed myself to be conned. I figured they knew what they were talking about since they went to college. I was uncomfortable in that world. I didn't know the rules. For the first time, I realized should have studied harder in school, maybe have taken a few business classes. But I didn't so I relied on my instinct, or what looked like a good deal. And I was wrong.

But, I did know the streets. I knew the gambling games, and I knew how to read gamblers, so I could win in that arena. People always go where they feel comfortable. Birds of a feather flock together, so I flocked right over to Louie's nest. We took up again as if nothing had happened. As if cooking and clothing stores was just a weird sidetrack, like a mini vacation in a trailer park, where you know sooner or later you will encounter aliens.

Louie's business had grown significantly, and he had bought a house and had a kid of his own. I went back to trucking, had the side games going again, and took on a night job as a watchman.

The side games, shylarking, and horse betting, were a nice nontaxable income. I was determined to get my family a house. That to me was the honest thing to do. How I did it seemed irrelevant, as long as I didn't hurt anyone and maintained my sense of humor. Practical jokes kept me going. I found out years later from my eldest daughter that I would get a certain gleam in my eye when I was playing a joke. Luckily, none of the guys had the urge to ever look that closely, and therefore never saw the jokes coming.

At the trucking company, Louie and I edged each other on.

Louie was exceptionally strong. He was able to handle freight that other guys would run away from. Louie had arms like Popeye after the spinach. I was strong, but not as strong. A man's gotta know his limits, or at least how to get around them. I would always challenge Louie with a gimmick in front of the guys—one that would pretend to test his strength, but be some parlor trick designed to turn bettors into losers.

My tests would aggravate him, and that would crack me up. One time I made him a bet that he couldn't hold his hand straight out with a small amount of weight in it for five minutes. I remember him looking at this tiny object, smirking at me, and saying, "You gotta be kidding me." However, he forgot to factor in gravity. Gravity works against you. Physically, you can't keep your hand up, not because of the object but because of the combined forces. It starts to feel too heavy. So he stood there holding his hand out, and after three minutes it started to sink. I started smiling, and he got mad. The more I smiled the madder he got. He chucked the weight to the ground and said, "I don't have time for your bullshit." But when the next time came around, he'd fall subject to my gimmicks again. Like all jokes and games of the mind, it's all in the wording.

I once said to him, "You can't hurt me with all your strength." I was still a boxer at heart and just being a man made me always feel the need to be competitive, no matter how childish. Actually, I didn't think it was childish, but I know women do. Men love challenging each other and given the chance, we'll bet on anything.

Anyway, Louie just nodded and walked away. Then he waited...like a jackal...to attack and embarrass me. He kept me on my toes for a few days, acting like he forgot what I said, and then he'd whack me on the ass with a two-by-four in front of the guys. He walked away laughing, "Now...we're even." My pride was temporarily scratched, but inside I smiled. Plotting my comeback. It's a guy thing. Just like Wrestlemania.

Look, men are animals. We know it. We love it. Sometimes we will even act more gross just to get a response out of you women. You want to really gross a woman out, fart in bed. Depending on the woman, sometimes you can get her to leave the bed altogether. I once did this to Nellie, she leaped so high and fast out of bed, I had to pry her from the ceiling. I don't know why but this made me laugh until I cried. Just make sure you do this *after* you make love, or you might find yourself sleeping alone on the couch with a deodorizer hung from your ass.

And another thing: Even though we tease, we do have feelings. We try to act macho, but it's all an image for ourselves, as well as others. When I was growing up, it wasn't cool to show your feminine side. You were considered a wuss. Today, if you cry you are "sensitive." But if you cry too much, you're still a wuss. You need a damn crying calculator to figure this shit out. I guess the point I'm trying to make is that the sensitivity was there, even in big burly guys like us truckers, you just had to look harder for it. We didn't wear our hearts on our sleeves. We modeled ourselves with the likes of Hollywood legends like Gable, Bogart, and The Duke.

Case in point. One day, the truckers over at Louie's decided we needed a mascot. We looked around the place and were inspired. We bought a small pig, named it Benny, and kept it in a pen in the trucking company. The guys would all feed it. Pigs are smart, too. We taught Benny all kinds of tricks, like how to open a beer can, how to fetch, and how to tug at a lady's skirt. Useful skills, I mean he was a male pig.

When Benny got too big, we decided the logical thing to do was to cook him and eat him. Logically, first we had to kill him. All these big, brave strong truck drivers didn't have the heart to kill Benny. Everyone made excuses why they couldn't do it. We decided to sell him. Before he left we had a going away party for him, took pictures of him in a party hat and with a cigarette dangling from his mouth. After Benny was sold, nobody mentioned him again. We were heartbroken. I really missed that pig.

I was still focusing on my goal of getting a house. When you have a goal, its amazing how little sleep you can go on. The adrenaline keeps you going. It's like a high. Not a lowlife drug high that fries your brain. I never believed in drugs; as a matter of fact I despised them and anyone who sold them, especially to kids. I mean, I drank Johnny Walker on occasion, and I was a heavy smoker, which was kind of the wise guy image thing to do. But adrenaline, if they could market adrenaline, that would be the thing to get. You wouldn't need anything else, that would keep you going. The way I see it, a goal is like dynamite, and adrenaline, that's the fuse that gets you there. You have a limited fuse so you use all your energies to get there to get the best impact.

Working three jobs, though, can also make you stunad (stupid). You do crazy things because you're dead tired. Your brain is fried, and you take on more than you can handle. You believe you are superman, without that stupid red cape.

This one afternoon at the trucking company, I told this guy, Sam, to roll the canvas on the truck by himself. We were short-handed and I'd seen Louie do it plenty of times. Sam said, "No way. Can't do it. Too heavy." I got mad. It was close to quitting time and I wanted to go home. I didn't need this ignoramus holding me up. I yelled at him, lost my temper, and fired him. I did the damn thing myself, or at least tried to.

The way to roll something depends all on leverage. Being I was short, I had to work out a system. I'd move a box by first rolling it, then putting the box down, then rolling it again. When I got to a certain point, I would have to step over the box. Stepping over the box backwards, I hurt my back. I was on the floor crying out in pain. Since I was always playing practical jokes, no one believed me. It was like the boy who cried wolf. All the truckers thought I was making fun of Sam. I'm saying, "OWWW, my back, my back." They just stood around laughing. An ironic joker's nightmare. Loving the laughs, hating the reasons. When they saw I didn't get up after a few minutes, they realized I was serious and took me to the hospital. Once again I found myself facing the homely breasts of a matronly nurse. This had to be some kind of payback from God.

You should have seen this broad. She was a big bull dyke-looking type. She looked like she'd be good in shot put or the javelin throw. I could picture her in a gym class wearing a big gray sweatshirt, towel around her neck, and pants a size too small where it looks like your ass is eating your pants. She was square like a refrigerator and had short hair and these heinous white, rolled up stockings. Her boobs were like missiles, and you could tell they would sag to her feet if she didn't have some anti-gravitational bra strap holding them up.

Luckily, my gorgeous Nellie came in to give my eyes a break. The nurse looked at her disapprovingly and left the room.

Nellie just shook her head as she stared at me in the hospital bed. "Frankie, when are you gonna learn?" She half grinned.

I smiled. "I did it for you?"

"For me?! How would I benefit? You're going to get yourself killed and you don't even have insurance money," she said sarcastically, then smiled.

"What, you're gonna blame a guy for wanting to spend some time with his wife and kid? I've realized I'd been working so much. I figured I'd get the work done quicker myself and then I could get home early and it, well, it backfired. Is Frannie here?"

"No, kids aren't allowed on this floor."

161

"What kind of stupid rule is that? Bent backs aren't contagious."

"Hey, I don't make the rules."

Just then the nurse from hell came back. "Okay, lights out. Visit's over. Get a move on, missy. I've got other patients to attend to."

"But I just got here."

"Not my problem. Hours are posted. Rules are rules. Good-bye."

"Hey, you don't have to be so nasty, lady," I said.

"Yeah, well, I'm not being paid to be nice," she snorted.

Nellie got up and kissed me on the forehead, and whispered. "See you in the morning." She walked out and left me with the devil's nursemaid.

The nurse handled me so roughly that a bout with an angry bull who had just been neutered would have felt better. Anyway, I fell asleep shortly after. Nurse 1, Frankie 0.

The next morning, I saw Nellie coming in with this devilish grin and a shopping bag.

"What did you get me?" I asked.

"It's a surprise. Precious cargo. A one-of-a-kind gift," she answered coyly. Then I heard a giggle. I peeked over and looked in the shopping bag. There in the shopping bag, underneath a Wandering Jew, was little Frannie peering up at me. Nellie had snuck our kid up to my room in a plant-filled shopping bag. Frannie jumped up as if caught in a game of hide and seek. "Here I am, Daddy. Don't I make a good Jew?" We all laughed.

I turned to Nellie and said, "And you thought I was crazy. I guess I'm not the only one who likes to break the rules?"

"Well, mister, this is an exception. You know I'm a by-the-book girl." She smiled.

"Don't I know it. I was praying by the big book every night while we were dating that you'd change that virgin rule."

"Frankie!" She pretended to slap me.

It was great seeing her and Frannie. Frannie jumped on me and only hurt my back once. Funny when a kid hurts you it still hurts but it feels a whole lot sweeter than if an adult clobbers you. Innocent pain. The visit ended when Nurse Breakass came walking down the hall, burst open the door, and we got caught red-handed.

"What the hell is all the laughing about?" Then she spotted Frannie. "Get that child out of here. You know the rules." For a moment there was silence we all looked at each other. Then I looked at the nurse's face. I glanced at Nellie. We burst out laughing. It was the kind of uncontrollable laughter that seizes you at inopportune moments. The kind of laughter you can't control even though you know it will get you into more trouble. The kind of laughter that makes you wish you were wearing a Depends. Frannie started to laugh, too.

Ever notice when you start laughing when someone's mad, it gets them even madder? It's like you are saying to them, "You look like an idiot getting mad. Your anger is not important to me, get lost." Well, the nurse turned about a hundred shades of red. It looked like her face was going to burst like a overly ripe pimple. Yes, a disgusting image, but that's what came to mind. Our refusal to have our spirits squashed made her furious. She leaped over to the bed and hovered over Nellie. Pointing to the door, she yelled, "Get out now! You broke the rules. No one breaks the rules when I'm in charge!" Steam was coming out of her nostrils.

Nellie smiled at her. "I get the feeling you want me to leave."

Nurse Breakass took on a Sumo wrestler pose and was ready to spring into action. Trying to calm her down, I said, "Listen, don't get your panties in a knot." Well, that sent her over the edge. Nellie got in between us before she broke me in half.

She reasoned, "Listen, just calm down. We get the point. We're leaving." She took Frannie by the hand, gave me a kiss good-bye, and headed towards the door. But not before I signaled Frannie to hit the nurse's butt on the way out. Frannie nodded her head, giggled, and did. Breakass was livid. Her head spun around like Linda Blair's head in *The Exorcist*. Her eyes were ablaze and she was making these guttural sounds. Nellie swooped Frannie up and out of spitting range. At the door she turned around and winked. Sometimes I can be very aggravating, but it was worth the laugh. Of course, I paid for it later dearly with Breakass. She was so angry at what we'd done, for the next few days I was flipped more times than a stack of pancakes. Good thing I had a lot of visitors, because she wouldn't do it in front of a witness. If she hadn't been a woman, and I use the term loosely, I'd have belted her.

In between visits from Nellie, my family stopped by to check in on me. My mom, God rest her soul, came mainly to see that I wasn't starving to death. She would sneak a basket of food in. Luckily, Breakass didn't see that. I could picture my mom smacking her with a loaf of bread. My dad would just stand at the edge of the bed and stare at me, like I was a lazy bum and did this on purpose. Teresa sent a Frank Sinatra poster and said, "It could have been worse." As for Vinny and Joey, they both said they were there if I needed them, then stuffed some money into my hand. How could two brothers from the same family be so different and so great at the same time? I admired and loved them both.

I was in the hospital for two weeks. I eventually got the nurse to smile—a feat that even St. Peter would have found challenging. Hell, I had to keep myself amused, and it was a matter of survival. If I could win over Satan's sidekick, the rest should be easy. Not to mention that I wouldn't get tossed around like a bad salad at a meat-eating convention.

As soon as I got out, crutches and all, I went back to work. I had a house to get, now more than ever...Nellie was pregnant again. I said I was convalescent, not crippled.

Everyone tried to discourage us from dreaming too big. They told us we were taking on too much. That we should wait a while, then buy a house in a few years. They gave us all the reasons not to move. Told us we couldn't come up with a down payment, the usual negative crap. It always amazes me how people are so negative about someone else's ideas. They have a million reasons why it won't work, or how they can do it better. Then if you succeed, they shrug and go, "Beginner's luck!"

Nellie, meanwhile, was studying hypnosis and this metaphysics stuff. She made me visualize every night that we were living in this nice, big house. I had never heard of visualization, and frankly, it sounded more like dreaming to me, but Nellie had explained it in such a way that it made sense.

She said, "Visualization is based on the principle that the subconscious mind doesn't know the difference between reality and what you picture to be reality. If you picture something in your mind and conjure up all the feelings associated with it, as if it really happened, your mind has no choice but to act as if this is reality because the mind accepts whatever you tell it as truth. Dreaming is passive. The key to visualization is to act as if it really happened and get your emotions and feelings involved. It's the same way your whole body reacts when you are in a haunted house at an amusement park. You know its fake, but for a moment you suspend reality and play along, then your heart beats faster, you start to sweat, you get jumpy, and even scream." Supposedly, Olympic athletics use this visualization thing in their training to win.

Anyway, at first I thought this was crap. Then I started to get into it. I figured that if some guy could use it to win a gold medal, I could use it to get a house. I could really see us in a nice, big house and feel how it would feel to own it. All my wise guy and trucker friends told me I was just daydreaming. After all, they were not the type to sit around the docks with a cigarette dangling from their mouths saying, "Ohm." It started to feel like witchcraft or something. What the hell did I know?

Nellie told me not to tell anyone what we were doing, that it works better that way. All I knew was that we were determined. Today nobody thinks twice of this New Age stuff, but back then it was considered weird and uncharted territory. People did it, they just didn't talk about it. It was something left for imaginations of fantasy writers of a B-rated flicks. With incense and candles to ward away any evil spirits, and mantras and chanting to get our bodies in tuned with the light, we really gave it our all. Nellie was also doing this to ensure another healthy baby.

Nellie had a thirst for knowledge. She was reading up on child psychology and wanted to get Frannie ready for a new addition to the family. She asked Frannie one day, "What would you like, a little brother or a sister?" After much thought, Frannie responded, "A dog."

So, we bought a dog. We figured we couldn't control what sex the baby would be, so let's appease the kid in the meantime. Nellie went out and got a freaking white little miniature poodle. We named her Gigi. I refused to walk this dog. Do you know how embarrassing it would be for a good-looking, almost wise guy like me to be seen walking a dainty little poodle on a leash? A poodle with bows no less. Talk about a blow to my image. But this little lady had a way; she licked my feet like Butch did and that took guts. Especially because somehow over the years, my feet turned into those "dad feet" with the gnarly toenails. And, they still stank, no matter how much spray I put on my feet. Any dog who could lick them without passing out was okay in my book. I wound up walking the pooch and gave dirty looks to anyone who dared sneer at me in the streets. The guys mocked me. Women thought it was cute. Eventually, just like anything else in the Village, no one noticed and I blended in.

Gigi was so much different than Butch, my childhood dog. Butch was much older now and still lived with my parents. Butch and I were buddies. I could play rough with Butch. Gigi was a little lady. I had to protect her. Totally different relationships, but I loved them both. Dogs are great. I wish people were more like dogs...loyal and low maintenance, no questions asked.

I walked the dog, worked three jobs, visualized with Nellie about our new house and baby, and got myself mentally ready for the next stage of life...more responsibility.

Nellie's stomach was getting bigger, and in September of 1964, Sherry popped out. Another beautiful baby girl. I was surrounded by women. The hospital bills set us back a bit, and the most ironic twist was that Nurse Breakass assisted our doctor in bringing Sherry into the world. Life sure is strange. Stranger still was that Nurse Breakass had a big smile on her face when she handed her over to Nellie and me, or maybe it was just gas.

No one is all bad or all good in life. We all dip into the other side at times—all of us. Just like Jeckyl and Hyde, it just depends which side of the bed you decide to sleep on. With me, I liked both sides and the sheets wrinkled.

Chapter Thirteen

Our little apartment was tight for the four of us. The time was getting near to leave Gendarmo's old apartment. We started to actively look for houses, even though we didn't have the money yet. We knew in our hearts that some way we'd get it.

We found a twenty-two-room English Tudor in Queens for a great price. It had a large backyard, brick fireplace, game room, parquet floor, humongous living room, and a finished basement. The owner had passed away, his children had moved out, and they wanted to unload the house. We called up a lawyer we knew, Dominic, and asked how long we could stall on a closing of the house if we left a fifty-dollar deposit. Yes, a fifty-dollar deposit, that's not a misprint. Dominic said he could stall it for a few months. We had hope.

I was working like a madman again, working three jobs; the trucking company, driving a cab, and on the side, as usual, shylarking and gambling. We had two months to accumulate $24,450, the balance of the down payment for the mortgage. It was getting close to the deadline. We were doing all that was humanly possible. I wasn't going to lose that house. I was the knight slaying the dragon. I had to win.

One night, the fever hit me again. I don't know if it was desperation, exhaustion, boredom with hard living, or frustration from getting things too slowly. Maybe it was just the Christmas spirit and wanting to play Santa. Whatever it was, I felt like a bloodhound tracking down his game.

I had my paycheck and was heading home and there it was—the distinct scent of a dice game in an alley. It seemed like destiny. I had to gamble. The devil and angel were on my shoulders battling it out. In the midst of their argument, I flicked them both off my shoulders and went into the game alone. I didn't need any distractions from the yakking of celestial beings. I mean, why would God put a dice game in front of me if I wasn't meant to play it? He knew I wasn't good at tests, so it had to be him just helping me out.

I watched for a few minutes as all the poor shnooks threw their money down in one last-ditch effort to play the hero at Christmas. I was about to join the ranks. It was like an invisible force was pulling me. I don't think I'm addicted to gambling, but I heard that all gamblers say that. And the truth is, if it is a disease, how come you can't deduct it as a medical expense?

Either way, I hadn't played for a while, but I always had the knack. I decided it was only one week's paycheck, let me give it a try. If I won, I'd be a hero, and we'd have a great Christmas. If I didn't, I'd be called a few names and sleep on the couch or worse, the fire escape. The truth is no wife likes a gambler, unless he's a steady winner. But I was feeling lucky, so it was worth a shot. Besides, the clock was ticking. There was only so long we could stall a closing. We had saved twenty thousand. We were so close.

I got into the game feeling I had to. It was the same rules as always, betting on the odds of "come" and "don't come." After ten minutes I was up three hundred bucks. After twenty, I was up seventeen hundred and fifty. At five thousand I stopped. I had just made the rest of the down payment on our new house.

I took the money, thanked the fellows, and walked away—carefully watching over my shoulder as I did. As Kenny Rogers said, "Know when to hold them, know when to fold them. Know when to walk away, know when to run." I was running on the inside to tell Nellie. Gambling once again had saved the day. How could something bad feel so good?

God works in mysterious ways. With all those chants, mantras, and visualization, craps in an alleyway won the day. Who knows, maybe the chants lead me to the crap game. I guess we'll never know.

I proudly walked into the house and said, "Nellie, get packed. All four of us. We are moving to Queens...Merry Christmas."

Her face lit up with both surprise and suspicion. Before she could get a word out, I picked her up and twirled her around, just like in those sappy movies. I can be real romantic at times. We celebrated, knowing Christmas that year was going to be great.

That night, after the kids were asleep, Nellie asked, "Frankie, what exactly did you visualize?"

I laughed, "What's the difference, it worked." No need blowing her incense-scented bubble.

We bought the house, but then we had no money to move. When in doubt, improvise. I got together all the truck drivers from the company, and we moved ourselves from our five-flight walkup in the Village to our Tudor in Queens. Thank God, we only had two rooms of furniture.

We were in by December 22. It was a proud day, moving into the house. I felt like a king being able to give my family this castle. Being the good Italian boy that I am, we took the extended family with us; Dad, Mom, Butch, and Nellie's brother Rudy came to live in the finished basement. The Waltons, or in our case the Waltonis, in Queens at Christmas—the more the merrier.

We loved the Tudor with its Spanish tiled roof. The dining room that could seat twenty-five comfortably was perfect 'cause we loved to entertain, and entertain we did.

Every weekend, Vinny and his gang and Joey and his clan would come on over. Moma would cook up some lasagna or manicotti, the kids would play together, and me and my brothers would catch up. Papa would just sit at the end of the table and nod as we spoke, as if he were overseeing the whole operation.

Vinny, of course, didn't talk much about work. Actually he didn't talk much about anything. He would always come in and say, "How ya doin'?"

Then I'd say, "Good. How you doin'?"

Then he'd say, "Don't ask." So we wouldn't. Then the same ritual would be repeated with my brother Joey, except he'd go into all the stuff he was up to. Then my brothers would turn to Papa and all he'd say was, "Eh, can't complain." Then we'd all play cards and Papa would drink a gallon of Gallo wine. As you can see, we weren't big on talking.

The women, on the other hand, would talk nonstop. They'd all bullshit together and do that women stuff like showing the house, talking about the kids, and helping Moma when she let them in the kitchen. The one thing you don't mess with is an Italian mom in the kitchen. It's like her holy sanctuary. God forbid you put the wrong ingredient in the sauce. Then you are responsible for ruining the whole dinner, and you have sit there and watch her wring her hands and plead to the Holy Family, "Jesus, Mary, and Joseph, my dinner, she's a ruined." Sometimes Nellie complained that it felt more like she was the guest and Moma owned the place. I gotta admit, it's not always easy living with an Italian mother-in-law.

After the first few hours I'd like to do magic tricks for the kids. There were seven kids by now: my two, Vinny had three, and Joey had two. Actually there was one more—this neighborhood kid, Georgie, always used to be at our house. Sometimes I thought we must have adopted him without my knowing.

Anyway, we'd take the kids downstairs into the finished basement. The basement was big, it had several rooms. I used to stand in front of the door at the bottom of the staircase that led to one of the rooms. I'd have the kids sit down, and I'd dim the lights all except for this one light that used to aim at the door, sorta made it look like a stage. I'd do all these magic tricks for them in front of this door, and then always ended it with a grand finale.

Little did they know that on the other side of the door was either Vinny or Joey, depending on the week. At an appointed time, I would say I was going to have a handkerchief float in the air, and one of my brothers would have a thin wire from the other side of the door all set up. I'd place the handkerchief on the invisible wire, and low and behold this thing would be swooping and diving, it was like...magic!

Other times, if I felt like scaring the hell out of them, I would tell them I was going to contact some dead relatives. I would tell them to hold hands like we were having a séance. Then I would tell the dead relative if they were in the room to let their presence be known.

Then one of my brothers would knock on the pipe or make some moaning sound. You never saw eight kids run up the stairs so fast.

We'd get yelled at by all the wives, "What the hell's the matter with you? Not one of you has a brain. You're scaring the kids!" We'd look at each other, then look at Papa, who didn't smile but had a gleam in his eye. But each week the kids would come around begging for me to do it again, "Oh come on, Uncle Frankie...please." So I did.

Nellie can't complain, she really was no better. She would put fake snakes or rubber spiders in the guests' rooms when they slept over. One year during New Year's, she went too far, though. She made a phony phone call to the police while the other wives listened. She said, "Hi, we're having a New Year's party and Guy Lombardo is here. Do you want to come and watch his balls drop?"

Vinny starting yelling at her, "What are you stupid, calling the police? Are you nuts?" I thought it was funny, but then again if I was Vinny, maybe I wouldn't have.

Anyway, the evening would always end with two things. First, I'd tell the ghost story of the "Golden Arm"—a story Joey told me when I was a kid, and which I loved to retell to see people jump. The story is about some wise guy kid named Johnny who lives with a rich aunt. The kid was always messin' around and one day he slammed an electronic iron gate on the old lady's arm and it got chopped off. She got it replaced with a golden arm. When she died she left everything to Johnny, except the arm. Johnny got in trouble gamblin' and dug up the arm The old lady's ghost came back to get it. The part I loved is at the end. I'd lower my voice to draw the kids in. I'd say it really spooky-like and keep repeating, "Whoooo's got my golden arm? Whoooo's got my golden arm?" When they least expected it, I'd raise my voice and shout, "WHOOOO'S GOT my golden arm!!" Every week the kids would jump, my moma would smack me on the head, and I'd laugh hysterically. I must have told that story a thousand times in my life.

At the very end of the evening we'd all go out in the backyard, except for my dad, and smoke. Joey didn't smoke either but he would join us. The backyard was our escape, for many reasons. One, it overlooked a pond so it was like having country living, with all the luxuries of the city. The other reason was my dad was getting older and used to pass gas more frequently, and man it stunk up the house. We would literally have to evacuate for about ten minutes into the backyard till the air was clear. That's the only time I really saw my dad laugh. At least we had that in common. The power of the gas. Men just find it funny.

It's just another guy thing. Me and Butch sometimes would stay in the house with him to prove we could—a sort of male bonding. My eyes would water. His farts could give tear gas a run for it's money. Sometimes I would tell the girls the coast was clear when it wasn't, and me and my dad would enjoy a second round of laughter.

The girls thought it was low-class, uncouth, and downright nasty.

Even Gigi seemed to agree. She'd stick her nose up in the air and turn proudly away. Dogs have their limits, too. I know people take offense to this. It's one of those things that is supposed to be done and not discussed. But that's what makes George Carlin so great. He discusses it all, no holds barred. Some of us like to think we're above it, but when it comes down to the nuts and bolts, we all take a shit everyday. Elvis died on the crapper. The difference lies in who discusses it. You think God cares? He's the one who invented this cosmic joke anyway.

Anyway, those were great times. That's what life's all about, family. Our Queens mansion allowed us to all get together comfortably.

Unfortunately, the mortgage was as big as the house, so we had to sacrifice some space and convert the upstairs into another apartment. We rented it to this nice Japanese couple with a kid. It was quite amusing seeing the wife, Tomoko, and Nellie talk for hours, even though they didn't understand a word each other was saying. I never understood that. I guess it's a women's thing, because Frannie and Tomoko's daughter did the same thing

Although I gotta tell you, those Japanese had a good sense of humor, too. One summer, everyone was over and it was hot. We had one of those above ground, quick assemble, metal pools in the backyard for the kids to cool off in. It was only about three feet deep.

I don't remember exactly what happened, but joking around, I threw Tomoko's husband, June, in the pool, with clothes on and everything. Tomoko came at me like a bat out of hell, "Ah, you no do that to my husband." Then she lifted me up like I was a fly weight and threw me in the pool. I yelled for Nellie, "You gonna let her do that to me?" Nellie nodded "yes" and started laughing. So, I got out and pulled her in. Then Tomoko started laughing and snapping pictures and June got out and pulled her in. Next thing I knew Rudy and Joey were diving in the pool.

Vinny just stood there nodding his head, "You're idiots. All of you." It was mayhem. The kids were all laughing watching the grown ups act like fools. We destroyed the pool.

Later that day, after everyone left, Tomoko was out in the backyard with June's wet wallet. One by one she removed the dollar bills and hung them up on the clothesline to dry. Very funny those Japanese.

189

Yeah, we were a little squished in, but we were living the American dream. Family, fixing up the house, working hard, house parties on weekends, but it wasn't enough. I didn't want to just get by, I wanted to be able to appreciate life on a grander scale and expand the dream. The way I saw it was, the greatest danger in life wasn't aiming too high and missing, it was aiming too low and reaching it. I didn't know what I wanted to do to get higher, but I was ready for opportunity to knock.

They say be careful what you ask for, because it will come true, and not always the way you expect it. One day this Danny Devito look alike—attitude and all—showed up at my door.

"Hi, my name is Ozzy. I'm your next door neighbor. I couldn't help notice you fixing your house up. You seem good with a hammer and nails. I'm in construction, and I'm looking to recruit a few good men. Interested?"

Interested! "Come on in, Ozzy. I think you and I are about to become good friends."

Chapter Fourteen

Over the next six months my life changed drastically. I left scamming with Louie Patooie. Louie went straight after a few run-ins with the tax man and took to concentrating solely on his trucking company. There just wasn't enough money in scams, and it was getting harder to hold onto the house. To try to make extra money, Nellie and I rented out the other half of the basement to this guy, Buddy.

Buddy was a little weird, but he was willing to pay top dollar. We never knew what he did for a living, nor did I ask. But every few weeks he'd have a different exotic animal at the house—just for a day or so. We saw otters, toucans, monkeys, koalas. A real zoo. The kids loved it. Buddy said he was taking care of them for a friend. What was his friend, a freaking zoo keeper? Rudy and Buddy had their own separate entrances. Nellie was getting a little agitated, feeling we had more of a boarding house than a home.

I threw myself into the construction work. I told Ozzy I didn't really know how to build, but I knew how to read blueprints and I was good with math. Ozzy had me manage, oversee, and hire the trades. This was good. I liked the job and got a feeling of accomplishment seeing the things go from scattered pieces of material to a finished product, as my business card said: "From concept to completion." I was leaving a permanent mark in the world.

In the meantime, death took over our house. Butch died. We found him one morning curled on top of my dad's newspaper. Ironically he was laying on a headline that read, "It's a dog's life." Nellie thought there might be some secret meaning there. I felt like it was God's way of making some kind of joke.

Either way, a member of my family was gone. We had a burial service, and the kids said prayers they made up for him. He lived a long time and was a great dog. There was an emptiness.

Then my dad died. His cough had been increasingly worse, and when he moved to Queens he couldn't do the peanut stand anymore. The lack of purpose killed him. It's weird when a parent goes. There are so many things now I wished I would have asked him. But you just didn't have those kind of discussions with your parents like that back then. It also makes you realize that we are all mortal. Even our mighty parents.

I was glad he got to see my house and be proud of me. That's all I ever really wanted, people to be proud and see that I could do it. Don't we all want that? To prove to ourselves that we can accomplish things and show the world that we are worthy in our own ways. For me, it boils down to laughter and being a good person.

If I can't find the humor in something, shoot me. No really, shoot me. Christ, you have to laugh. I laughed when others cried, not out of malice, but with how funny situations just come about naturally. So without missing a beat, I found the humor in my dad's funeral.

The funeral was something out of an old cops and robbers movie. My brother Joey was a cop now and living in Brooklyn, and Vinny, well, Vinny was making money on the other side of the law. Both of them were highly respected in their chosen circles. But ironically, because of being in direct opposition, they knew each other's friends. To show respect for our family, the friends from both corners of the law came. The Police Lieutenant came, as did the Capo di Tutti.

The timing of the visits couldn't have been planned better than if it were a high-society debutante dance. As the crooks came in, the cops went out. Cops in, crooks out, crooks in, cops out. A funny waltz with

195

unlikely partners. They came through different doors. Poetically the police came thorough the front, the crooks through the back.

Some of the people from Vinny's gang were wanted by the police, but the police didn't do anything at the funeral, because it was a place of sanctuary. They looked across at each other, nodded, and quickly made an exit. My mom was oblivious to the whole thing and was amazed how many friends Papa had. "I didn't know your father knew so many well dressed people!"

The whole scene looked like a cartoon to me. People's heads peeking in and popping out if the right element wasn't there. No one else saw the humor in it. Maybe I'm just weird, but I feel if I can laugh at something later, why wait? I might as well just laugh now. I laughed till I cried.

Chapter Fifteen

With Dad gone, Mom decided to move to Florida and live with Teresa and her husband. Off she went like a good elderly person to Florida. What is it about that state that draws the elderly like magnets? They have flying roaches the size of New York City rats! They call them palmetto bugs, as if changing the name makes it any better. Either way, Mom was out. The house was losing its occupants quickly.

For the first time, my house really felt more like my castle, even though I barely was home. I picked up the construction work quickly, and Ozzy had a lot of rich clients who wanted rooms added on, closets built, garages finished, and other odds and ends. I liked this job a lot. Things were going well. Maybe I could make it straight after all. I knew I'd miss the lure of being on the edge, but it was the money that counted in the end.

I felt I had a grip on all of this. I was home less, and I guess I ignored Nellie and the kids somewhat—all right, a lot. The curse of fatherhood. The more you work to make their lives better, the less you know your family. It's a cruel exchange program, but the accepted way of life, then anyway. Nowadays everybody's trying to find the balance of work and personal life. I figured my moma accepted it, why shouldn't Nellie?

I think I should have listened closer, though. One night, Nellie said she couldn't take it anymore. She didn't want to live in a house with a drug addict. I didn't know what the hell she was talking about. Turns out Buddy was a pusher. The sick thing was he transported the drugs in the body cavities of the animals. How sick is that? And what sick person would want to take the drugs after they've been in some monkey's ass?

Anyway, one night Buddy wasn't home and one of the monkeys was making noise. Nellie went down to check because the creature was extremely loud. When she opened the door, it was like a jail cell had been sprung open. Then animal leaped over her, ran through the kitchen, jumped out the window and escaped into the park. Nellie tried to coax the monkey back, but freedom was much more attractive. Who knows, maybe he had his own drug connections, selling it to the squirrels, those hyper little rats with tails.

When Buddy came home he saw the monkey was gone, he asked Nellie, and she told him what had happened. He flipped out. She told him, "Why don't you just call the police and fill a missing monkey report?"

He grabbed her by the shoulders and started shaking her. "Did you call the police? DID YOU?" Nellie, realizing he was going nuts and not sure what to answer, said, "No, I didn't."

"Do you know what you have done? Do you know what you have cost me?" He started yelling. "Do you want me to take your stupid poodle?" The kids started crying and screaming. Nellie sent the kids to their room and told them to shut the door. She managed to talk Buddy down, but it took a while. Finally, he stormed out of the house, but not after smacking her in the head and kicking the dog. The kids heard Nellie crying and the dog whimper.

Nellie called me the second he left. I found Buddy and had to bust his head open for this. Made things messy. But you don't lay a finger on my family.

Nellie had told me several times before that she thought he acted weird. I thought she was just annoyed at having another tenant. I ignored her and told her, "It's your overactive imagination. The guy is fine." He always acted fine when I was around, but when I was away, Buddy would call. I had to stop this. So I did. I didn't kill him or anything. But there are ways to let people know you mean business. And when they mess with your family, the game is up.

Nellie blamed me for bringing the trash into the house, never being home, missing the kids' school plays and such. But mostly she blamed me for never listening to her. She warned me about Embezzlement Nancy. She warned me about Buddy. She warned me about certain friends. I just shrugged her off. After all, I was the man of the house.

She wanted to get a divorce. I never even saw it coming. As with most couples, one is always blinded to the effects that they have on a relationship. You think everything is fine because you are working your butt off. But you never take time to discuss it and see the effects it has on the other partner. No one's to blame. Both are to blame. Doesn't matter, the results are the same...divorce.

Chapter Sixteen

We stayed in the same house till I could make other arrangements. Hard to believe I'd come all this way just to get divorced. What else can happen now? I realized, looking back on life, that you should never ask a question you don't want the answer to. God showed me what else could happen. One night while we were all out shopping, the house caught fire. They said the boiler in the basement exploded. We came home to a house engulfed in flames.

We spent the night across the street at a neighbor's. We watched from their attic window as our house went up in flames. We watched as the firetrucks came. We watched as fire shot out the windows and curtains formed columns of flames. We watched as the soul of the house dimmed down with the last douse of water. To outsiders it was just another house. To my family, it was the end of a dream. The blackened house now stood there, with faint smoke rising and disappearing, as my dream of a happy family and the American dream had died at the same time.

The next day, all that was left was rubble. What the fire hadn't damaged, the water from the firehoses did. I don't know how much it takes to break a man's spirit, or why we are tested in strange ways, but something changes, something hardens in your soul to let you go on. With each experience, hopefully a lesson is learned. Sometimes you just have no clue of what the lesson is, and all you can feel is the pain.

We temporally moved into the Courtyard Hotel in Jamaica, until I could figure out what to do. The divorce was put on hold till we could regroup. We stayed there for a few weeks till I found an apartment in Jamaica Estates. I moved Nellie, the kids, and Gigi in. The dog had been shopping with us that night, a last minute plea from the kids to take the dog with us ever since she had been kicked. I stayed at Ozzy's for a while.

I was still doing construction, and I missed my boxing days. I was working on a forty-house FHA job in South Jamaica for a friend of Ozzy's, Lenny Lipman, a millionaire.

Lenny and I hit it off because we both had a love for boxing. At one time, Lenny was the boxing manager for this black kid named Elroy. He lost his client when Elroy went to jail for armed robbery. When Elroy came out, he was in good shape. He tracked down Lenny and still wanted to fight.

Lenny said, "Hey Frankie, want to get out some aggression? Why don't we see if the kid's got anything left in him. Jail may have honed his killer instinct." Being as I used to be a boxer, I was game. I got my trainer's license and was ready for my first client.

I started to train Elroy at Stillman's Gym in downtown Manhattan. Elroy looked good in the gym.

Before he went to jail, he once fought Mohammed Ali when he was still known as Cassius Clay. He gave Clay a good fight, but he lost. I figured I'd give him a shot, anyway.

First, I tested Elroy. I wanted to see him run, not jog, for half an hour straight. Then I would know if he had the stamina to last the rounds before I would even consider taking him on. I made him do laps around the construction site. He was able to do them with ease. So I took him on.

I worked with Elroy for about three months. As a trainer I made him go to the gym three days a week. In addition, I made him work on construction five days a week. This way he'd make money, work out, and stay out of trouble at the same time. Three intense hours at the job.

I observed him in the gym to check his style and see where I could improve on his technique. I didn't like his routine so I changed it. He was trying to be too

205

much like Mohammed Ali. The only problem was, Elroy didn't have the class, the swiftness, or coordination for it. I tried to change him into a puncher.

There are two types of fighters. A boxer and a slugger. A boxer uses finesse like Jack Robinson, Mohammed Ali, and Tommy Hearns. A boxer jabs, uses a right cross, a faint, a hook...all the mechanics of boxing. A boxer will avoid getting hit and hit you with a punch.

A slugger or puncher like Tyson and Marciano will go in and take a punch to hit you with a punch. A slugger is closer to a street fighter. A guy like Joe Lewis was both a puncher and a boxer.

In my opinion, the best heavyweight fighter of all time was Mohammed Ali, and Rocky Marciano was the best slugger who went undefeated in his career, 49-0. Although I heard he was a cheap prick. Supposedly, when he died, he left behind no will, no insurance and little in assets, and somewhere out there was a million bucks of his floating around. One time he went to the movies with his daughter and stashed a brown bag under the seat while they watched the movie. Rocky forgot about the bag, but his daughter remembered and handed the bag to her dad. In it was forty thousand bucks in cash. Rocky hated banks and always kept cash hidden, that cheap skate...you can't take it with you.

Anyway, who am I to comment on a person's lifestyle? I liked the challenge of making a good fighter out of someone. It reminded me of the days when I fought, and it was a break from the construction and a distraction from the divorce. The best way to forget something is to replace it with something else. That's the way I was brought up. Today's shrinks want you to go over and over what happened till you're sick of hearing yourself talk. It's like picking at a scab, the damn thing's trying to heal and you keep reopening the wound. I just wanted to move on and forget about it. It may not be the best way, but it was the best way I knew how.

I put my heart into making a killer schedule for Elroy. I made him punch the heavy sand bag for half an hour to put strength behind the punches. Then I'd make him use the light bag for swiftness and timing. I taught him how to hold and hit. It's an illegal move that I learned from years of survival in street fights, but it works. The trick is to not get caught doing it. I showed him how to be sneaky holding and hitting by holding the wrist or the cup of the arm of the other guy, or purposely missing the opponent and then hitting him with the elbow and then quickly follow up with a punch with the other hand.

I taught him all the sneaky and dirty tricks of fighting, but to no avail. He didn't win any fights outside of the gym. When the head gear was off, he ran away like a little sissy. It was embarrassing. With head gear on, he was a tiger. The head gear was his security blanket. He might as well have sucked his thumb and shit his pants. He couldn't handle it psychologically.

Three months of training and the first fight he had outside the gym he panicked. He lost in his first fight in four rounds. Believe me, the guy he was fighting was a dog. I could've beat the guy myself. Elroy lost it, and I ditched him.

After the fight I was disgusted. It seemed like one disappointment after another. Sure, I got the house, married, and made lots of money over the years, but I wanted it to stay on the upswing. Who doesn't? This was for the birds. Sometimes you just can't wait till life gets better so you can start really living, and then you turn around and realize, this is life. Then you have to look at what is good. At least the construction was going good. But it was time to move on, I decided. I was getting a little tired of living with Ozzy and his family and I'm sure they felt the same about me.

I went to a local bar to clear my head. Ain't that a laugh. We say "clear our head" with alcohol, while it doesn't really do that at all. Occasionally it does seem to lift your spirits, though, which is exactly what I needed. A drink now and then can't hurt. Just don't become dependent on it. That's where you get into problems.

I was at The Eight Wonders Restaurant on Queens Boulevard. I knew the bartender, Alex, from way back when I used to live on Sullivan Street in Manhattan. Alex and I were shooting the breeze. Catching up on old times, talking about the fight that Elroy had just lost, scores on ball games, what women call typical male bull. Then we started to play one of our favorite bar games, liar's poker.

Bar-style liar's poker is simple. You take out a one-dollar bill. You say one of the serial numbers off your bill. Let's say you say, "I got two nines." Then the next person says he's got three nine's, etc.

Whenever you feel the accumulation of numbers exceeds the numbers that was actually on the bill, you challenge that person. If he doesn't have what he claimed to have, he gives you his money. If he does, then you give him your money.

After a few rounds, we moved on to strength contests by picking up chairs and holding just one leg to see who was stronger. This guy named Mark Stein, Alex's friend, wanted to get in on the games. He was a steelworker, six foot one, slender, with dark, tight curly hair, no scars, heavy eyebrows that would make Brooke Shields cringe, and a big nose.

He was a Jewish guy, and us Italians get along famously with the Jews. He was also a strong, I mean "strong," guy. He won the chair contest, no problem. I challenged him to arm wrestling. I won. After all the games that men play were done, we sat down and had a drink.

I mentioned that I needed an apartment. Mark had an apartment that he was watching for his mother, so I moved out of Ozzy's house and into a long, fun-filled adventure of singledom with Mark.

Chapter Seventeen

Mark and I got along because we both had a warped sense of humor. We'd think strange things, challenge each other to crazy bets, and then go through with them. We were both divorced and reliving our second bout with sowing our oats.

The first thing we decided to do was change the decor of his mom's apartment. She said to "watch" the apartment for her, not leave it untouched. So we watched it change into our own creation. We were bringing women home. We needed a place that reflected our style. Something different that they would remember.

We got very creative. We took all the furniture out of his mom's bedroom and painted the walls black. We drew furniture on the walls, and painted them in with glow-in the-dark paint. We drew a complete bedroom set; dressers, night tables, a headboard, we even painted a lamp and had a light bulb sticking out of the wall so you could turn it on. A three-dimensional drawing. It would have been easier to get real furniture, but that would have interfered with our master plan. Instead of carpet, we covered the entire bedroom floor with mattresses. It was one big bedroom, and the floor was one big bed. The best part was, every time a girl would step into this room, she would trip not knowing there was a step made from two mattresses. Immediately she'd fall and be lying face down on the bed. Everyone got a kick out of the room. After all, if the girls were coming home with us late after the bar, they weren't expecting to play pinochle. Mark and I had many wild times in there. But I'm not one to kiss and tell.

We were like Oscar and Oscar living together. Neither of us liked housework. Mark didn't understand how I always got my end done. I told him my secret was I got my girls to do it. I would sweet talk the women into helping me by telling them I was divorced, a hard worker, and the rest of the "poor me" sob story. They would offer to help. I loved it. I'm a great cook. I'd offer to cook them a meal, if they'd clean up. It seemed like a fair exchange.

Mark soon caught on, and the two of us were living like kings. Sometimes if we got bored, we'd put all the girls' names we knew in a bowl—his black book and mine combined. Whatever name we fished out of the bowl, we had to call up. Other times, we would try to pickup each other's girls to see if they would go along with it. Yeah, sleazy men games, but every guy does it. Any girl who wants to fool herself into thinking her man isn't thinking with his small head ninety percent of the time is just fooling herself. I mean, don't get me wrong, men do fall in love. But at that time, we weren't in that head. No pun intended. As far as I was concerned, I was never getting married again. I had two great kids that I loved. I had no need to get married ever again.

Now, some of our antics got us into trouble. For example, let's say a wise guy's girl would come onto us. We didn't know who she was dating, so we'd take her home. Then at two in the morning some pissed off wise guy would come banging on the door and you'd have to scram out the back window like a common crook. Hopefully, you had time to put your clothes on; otherwise you ended up standing outside in your shorts like an asshole, trying to run and put your pants on at the same time.

But I wouldn't have traded it for the world. Living life on the edge was a rush. I just wanted to have fun, make money, and enjoy life.

I knew more than Mark about the ways of the street and fighting. More times than not, Mark couldn't see a fight coming till the fist was in his face. I'd just shake my head and say, "You never learn, do ya?" It started to become a bad habit. Mark felt I was his personal bodyguard, and often his liquid courage got us into trouble.

This one night, we went out of our neighborhood into a different bar in Queens. Mark approached this blonde, big-bosomed broad and asked if he could buy her a drink. The girl got all flirty and started curling her hair and making goo-goo eyes. It was ridiculous. Marks was beside himself and couldn't get the bartender's attention fast enough. I could tell he wasn't thinking with the ten percent of his head. The bartender obviously knew something Mark didn't know because he was purposely ignoring him. I watched this whole thing out of the corner of my eye. Just as I was going to go over to Mark to tell him something didn't seem right, this big guy came over, got in Mark's face, and said, "Stay away. She's my girl." The girl, obviously drunk, said, "Don't listen to him, sweetie, he's a liar. He doesn't own me. No man owns me." She gave a cold stare to the supposed boyfriend". I'm expecting Helen Ready to walk in singing, "I Am Women Hear Me Roar." Whenever a broad starts talking that crap, there's gonna be trouble.

No one moved for a second, and then Bright Eyes turned to Mark and said, "And besides I think you're cute."

That's all Mark had to hear. Now with his ego boosted and liquid swirling in his veins, he yells real loud to the guy, "Piss off." I started to see the local crowd gathering, like politicians to a sex scandal.

"Hey Mark, the natives are getting restless," I whispered.

Mark ignored me with his scotch-filled veins. He repeated himself louder this time to Jumbo, "You heard the lady. She likes me...now piss off."

By this time everyone was waiting to see what would happen. The big guy got even closer to Mark's face, kissing distance, and said, "Who you telling to piss off, pal?"

At that point, Mark looked him square in the eyes and said, "You know, your breath stinks."

I stepped in quickly even though I knew I'd had a few too many drinks to really have a clear head. I hated fighting when I was drinking, because I wasn't as quick and ended up doing stupid things. I tried to get Mark out of there. He wasn't going. He hadn't gotten laid in a few weeks, and he was thinking with the wrong head, filled with the wrong liquid. Before I could pull Mark away, the guy popped him right in the face.

Now, there's one thing you don't do, and that's hit a friend of mine. Right or wrong, I'm beside you if you're my friend. I put down my drink and swung back at the guy, hitting him first in the face, and then a follow-up to his chest. It started a full-swing bar brawl.

I remember getting picked up and tossed out. Like a bulldog, I huffed, brushed myself off, and ran back in to save Mark. Before I could get to where he was, I was whacked over the head with a bar stool. Let me tell you, it's nothing like in the movies with the cracking wooden sound. It's more like a loud thud. Lucky, I have a hard head. Nothing fifteen stitches couldn't fix.

I was dazed for a moment, but I quickly thought enough to pick up a bottle and crack it over the nearest guy's head. Misery loves company. I no longer knew who was fighting who. Arms were flying, people were ducking, glasses were cracking, women were screaming, and all the while in the background "I Did it My Way" by Frank Sinatra was playing. He was always around when some part of me was either getting taken out or broken.

Before I knew it, I got thrown out again, and again I went back in. It was like a bad cartoon fight where all you see is one blurry, frenzied rolling ball of people. Then all of a sudden it stops and the character realizes he's just fighting himself while the other guy is leaning on a tree or something watching nearby. I realized I couldn't see Mark. The blonde broad who started all this caught my eye and signaled with her finger that he was out the door. I went outside and there was Mark dusting himself off.

"What the hell you doing out here?" I asked.

"I thought you had left. I went back in and didn't see you so I came back out," he replied a little more sober now.

"I went back in and got a stool over my head for you."

We both peeked back in the bar. They were still fighting, unaware that we were gone. Mark put his arm over my shoulder, shook his head, and said, "That was stupid, huh?" I had to agree. We walked home laughing and bloody. Male bonding. I miss those good times.

Chapter Eighteen

Mark and I decided it was best to hangout at Eight Wonders. We had met some pretty nice girls there, and there was always a new supply. Plus, the music wasn't so loud that you had to scream at someone to be heard.

I went out with this one redhead for a while. She was a lot of fun, but I really wasn't ready to have a serious relationship. It lasted for a while. She was a good girl, still married though to this guy who she hadn't lived with in over ten years. Never got around to divorcing him.

This one night after work, Mark and I were drinking heavily. Whenever Mark and I had too much to drink we'd come up with these really stupid, embarrassing bets.

We made a bet that whatever song played on the jukebox we'd take turns acting out the title of that song. If you couldn't act it out, you had to sing it loud enough for the whole bar to hear. If you didn't, you lost. Something about drunks singing is funny. It was the forerunner to Karaoke. If we only had thought of adding a mike and lyrics, we'd be millionaires.

We tossed a coin, and Mark was up first. Mark acted out "Run-Around Sue" by putting a hat on his head, running around the bar, and batting his eyes. The guy was nuts. Here was this big steelworker acting like a fool. That's why I loved that guy. I was a little too cool for that. I've been known to do things, like dress up a blow up doll and bring it to my brother's birthday party, but personally, I couldn't run around and bat my eyes. Some things, even when drunk, I wouldn't do.

It was my turn up at bat. I saw this gorgeous blonde walk up to the jukebox. I figured I would use my charm and persuasion to get her to play an easy song. "Hey miss, could you do me a favor? Be careful what you play on the jukebox. My friend and I have a bet, and I have to act out whatever song you play."

She thought about it then played "I'll Never Cry Again." I said, "Ah. My theme song." I stood there and pointed to my face. "Look no tears!" I winked at her and gave her a nod. Mark said, "What the hell was that...look no tears? That sucked. You lose, pay up."

I didn't care. I had my eyes on the blonde. I sent her over a drink. She played it cool and just thanked me with a nod. Why is it I love the ones that play hard to get? Don't I ever learn?

About half an hour later, I saw somebody trying to pick her up. She looked annoyed, so I intervened. This was my chance to play a knight in shining armor—a role I liked to play. She seemed to like the rescue maneuver. Her name was Deidra. I got her number and thus began my second long-term relationship.

Chapter Nineteen

Once again I had a steady girl. I was trying the balancing act. I saw my little girls on weekends. I was still doing construction, at the time contracted to build a chain of fast food places, and was on good terms with Nellie. I was staying straight. Things were good.

I heard that my brother Vinny had just made a big score, and about a hundred grand was his share. Not that you would know it by looking at him, 'cause he was real careful to keep a low profile, but word has a way of traveling. To make matters worse, my brother Joey had arrested some of Vinny's friends, but they were released because there wasn't enough evidence. I wasn't even sure if he knew Vinny was involved, and I sure as hell wasn't going to go poking my nose into their business.

Mark and I were still hanging out at Eight Wonders. We had a routine now. We would go there in the early evening before it got too crowded and bullshit with the regulars.

This one day, it was only Alex, the bartender, me, and Mark in there. The regulars hadn't arrived yet. Alex was bitching that he needed money. He was always bitching about money, but this time he was really crying poverty. If there's one thing I hate, it's a crybaby. He was saying that his job just didn't pay enough to make ends meet. Mark and I started giving him ideas on some possible side jobs. He kept shooting every idea down.

Finally, kidding around, I said, "You want money? Rob a bank. That's where the money is. Bank robbery is the easiest thing to do. Cops don't respond in less than five minutes. If you could go into a bank and do the job in less than five minutes, you should be able to get away clean, then you'd have your money and I could get a drink without hearing you whine." He just stared at me. I could see he thought I was serious. I'd thought he could tell by the gleam in my eye that I was kidding. I started laughing at him. "I had you going didn't I?"

He was too quiet. I could hear the rusty wheels in his head grinding. Then he started nodding his head, "I like it, Frankie. I like it."

Mark looked at me and shrugged. "Alex, you jerk. He was kidding."

"I'm not," he replied. Then he started to ramble like an eager kid a Christmas, "Look Frankie, I have the balls to do it. You don't have to be in on it, just tell me how you would do it. I mean you look like the type that's done it. You look like you could be a wise guy or something." I didn't know whether to smack him or be complimented.

"First of all, stop your yakking. You're talkin' out of your ass. I'm in construction, and I'm totally legit."

"Sorry, Frankie. I just thought you could tell me how you would do it? Hypothetically."

I was always good with on-the-spot quick solutions, and I figured the guy meant no harm so I said, "Okay. Hypothetically speaking, if I was to rob a bank, I would need three men and a getaway car with a driver. The three men go into the bank. One man with a shotgun covers the bank. The other two men jump over the counter and clear the drawers of cash. Don't wait for the tellers to give you the cash, push them away, and take the cash. Don't worry about them setting off alarms. You go in and out in three minutes. How's that for on-the-spot planning?"

"Thanks, Frankie, you're all right." He smiled and poured me and Mark a drink. "This one's on the house." We all drank up. The regulars started coming in and I thought nothin' more of it. I didn't want to know.

A week later, Alex approached me when Mark wasn't around and told me he had two other people interested in this type of operation and would I set it up

229

for him? I told him he was nuts. But the more he talked, the more I could picture the job. Then I thought about my brother's big score, and before I knew it, I was agreeing to help him.

I wasn't sure how the hell I got roped back into this. I mean, do people attract these things in their lives as tests!? God knows, I hated tests and never did good on them. But I was always a sucker for figuring out a puzzle when it presented itself. Throw in some money and adventure, and I was hooked. I thought it over and my mind started churning.

I told him that I'd tell them what to do, but that I didn't want to know when, what bank, or the details. I instructed them to go to the bank and make a map of the layout. Be specific, I warned. Look at all the details. How many guards? Who opens up? What time does he come in? How many doors? Where are the tellers? What kind of alarm system? When do the employees arrive? Can outsiders see you from the street? I stressed the importance of him doing his homework thoroughly. All this coming from a high school dropout. Proves you only really learn when you want to.

Within a few days Alex came to me with a blueprint of the place. All the details were there. It was like a script.

"If this were the place, what would you do?" he asked, luring me in farther. It was like giving sweets to a diabetic. They crave it even though they know it can kill 'em.

I studied the layout and played along with this game.

"If I were doing this, I would rehearse the robbery in a separate place, just like an actor would do for a movie. Practice timing, your jumps, who is where, who is clearing the drawers, who is covering the door. Makeup scenarios of what if's. What can go wrong and what you would do. In other words be a good Boy Scout. Be prepared."

Alex just nodded with a gleam in his eye. "That's all?"

"One final touch," I added, "I would use a chain and a lock when leaving the bank. If you put a chain with a lock on the doors as you leave, no one could get out, and the police can't get in without a cutter. It gives you added time to get away. That's how I would write the scene."

A few weeks later, Alex mentioned that he had come into money. I got a free drink and a slight director's fee. We toasted to Hollywood.

Chapter Twenty

People are drawn to different professions because there are things in their personalities that make them good at it, or because they are naturals. Certain personalities go hand in hand with career choices. Accountants are usually laid back, rational, logical, are good with numbers, and get satisfaction out of working with the system and making it work. Attorneys are usually aggressive, like the fight, and take the big money.

I liked finding ways to get around the system. There was also something alluring to me about doing something you weren't supposed to do and beating the odds. Too bad they didn't pay guys like me to show them what's wrong with the system. Then I could be on both sides at the same time.

All I know is people get kicks out of different things. Some people get that adrenaline flow from bungee jumping or scuba diving with sharks. I got the thrill when I would mastermind a plan, see it through, and not get caught. It's the same rush I got with gambling, except I wasn't as in control with the roll of the dice, even though I had my own system like any good gambler.

There's glory in masterminding a plan and it working. When Alex approached me again a few months later, I was game. The same trio was assembled, and they decided to pull a different robbery.

Like Robin Hood and his gang of merry men, we went after only institutions or the rich. First we had to pick our targets. Like any lion waiting in the bushes of Africa and spotting his prey, we'd study a potential victim's weak points. Which way will it run? Is it fast, or will the prey come down easy?

One subject was a rich Jewish woman on Queens Boulevard wearing a mink fur coat and diamonds that would make King Tut proud. We followed her home. Hell, an animal rights person would have attacked her right there and taken the coat.

We were after something different. We figured that if she wore the coat and jewelry everyday, her home must be loaded. We jotted down where she lived and began finding out about the broad. We found out she was the wife of a doctor, a proctologist. Why a man would want to grab another man's balls, I'll never understand. A gynecologist I could understand because at least you get a better view.

Anyway, whatever he was staring at, he was bringing in a lot of dough. And he had expensive taste, too. Art work, antiques, you name it, he collected it. We learned both their schedules, so we would know the best time to attack. Again I laid down the plans, and the guys, seasoned actors now, followed the instructions.

The plan was simple. Always strive for simplicity, less things can go wrong. I told them to knock on the door and say that they were selling magazine subscriptions for a charity. When she opens the door, go in and take what you want. Calm her down, be polite, talk, don't yell. We didn't want to give the woman a heart attack. Ask her where the good stuff is and be courteous. Tell her it will be over soon. Lock her in the bathroom. Pull the phones out.

Life is ironic and some things don't go as planned. Some go better. The guys did the hit, then came over and told me what happened.

"Frankie, you're not going to believe this," Alex said.

"Before you start, you didn't hurt the lady, did you?" I asked. "After all I have a mother and I'd feel the need to kill any bastard who'd laid a finger on her."

"Don't worry, the woman was left unhurt and happy. Turns out her ole man, Doc Peters, was cheating on her."

"With another woman?"

"No better, with some of his clients."

"Get out of here. That's sick. The guy was a snake charmer?"

"Bingo. Up the ole yin yang. She had been trying to figure out a way to get back at him for years. She had felt demeaned as a woman. Said she could handle it if it had been another woman, but the insult of it being a man lowered her self-esteem. She was so miserable she was even considering suicide till we showed up."

"How the hell did you guys find all this out? You were doin' a robbery, not a social call."

"Frankie, we walked in like you told us. She let us in no problem. We told her to relax, and that it was a holdup and that we just wanted a few things and she wouldn't get hurt. Then she just looked at us and started laughing. We got all nervous at first, and then she starts laughing and yelling, 'Oy...Oy, this is too good to be true. God has answered my prayers. He works in mysterious ways, he does.' And she keeps laughing. Then she says, 'You boys couldn't have come at a better time, and to think I don't have to pay someone to do the job.' Frankie, we didn't know what to make of her. We thought maybe she was yanking our chain or something. Then she goes into this whole long story about her tight ass husband who's been cheating on her for the past five years with the male clients and to try to compensate he buys her all these gifts, mostly famous art statues and paintings of naked men. At first she thought it was for her, but then she realized he was getting pleasure looking at them. Frankie, I tell ya it was sick. She was too embarrassed to tell anyone in her circle of friends. She was thinking of setting fire to the stuff he liked, or drawing boobs on the naked men just to piss him off. But she couldn't get herself to ruin good artwork, said it was in her blood. So me and the boys are saying, 'Lady that's all fine and good but we don't need to hear your life story. Just go in the bathroom and quit your yapping and we'll be out of here.' Then she says, 'You boys don't get it. This is your lucky day. I want you to take all his prized possessions. Here's his baseball collection, his silver medals, signed golf clubs, gold watch, diamond cuff links, stash of cash. Oh and I guess you better take a fur coat or two of mine and this stupid antique broach from his mother. I hated his mother. Frankie, she went around the house like Santa Claus filling up our bags. It was the weirdest thing in the world. She even offered us coffee, but we declined."

"Geez, surprised you guys didn't offer to bake cookies with her," I said sarcastically. "So how'ja leave it?"

"Well, she told us to tie her up to make it look good. She even told us to remember to wipe our prints off of everything. Frankie, I know this is going to sound nuts. But I liked that broad. I felt like kicking the doc's ass for hurting her."

"The Doc may of liked it! You guys are nuts, though, making friends with the victim. This sounds like stuff out of a movie."

Movie or not, half the stuff we couldn't get rid of without causing suspicion, like his silver medals. We had to melt those down. But the coats, cuffs, and collector's stuff was a gold mine.

The next step was unloading the merchandise. Getting a buyer. One of the trio said he knew a guy, Bert Z., who bought swag. That's the lingo for stolen stuff. We contacted Bert Z. via phone and made arrangements for him to come look at the stuff and offer a price. We arranged a meeting place at night, near a section of the local park where no one usually ventured. We sold the stuff to him for twenty thousand dollars. We were happy till later we found out through the underworld grapevine that he gypped us, he didn't even give us the swag price.

Now, I know you are probably thinking, how the hell can we feel cheated when it wasn't even our stuff to begin with? Serves us right. But the way we saw it, we did a job, we helped out an old lady who was practically a silent partner, and we wanted to get paid the right price. The dealings in the underworld might be twisted, but a similar code of ethics as in the legit world applied. You get paid overtime if you stay late. A job should bring a certain fair market price. The code is, we are supposed to get an honest—there's an ironic choice of words—price.

Bert Z. now became the enemy. We had to get even. We planned our revenge. We got our guy to tell Bert Z. a week later that we had more stuff, an even bigger load. Bert Z. came driving up in his brand new

Cadillac with that stupid smirk on that says, "You assholes, this is going to be like taking candy from a baby." He strutted over with his sidekick. But this time we were on to them.

"Okay, where's the stuff?" he says, trying to sound important.

"Right here, asshole." And I punched him in the stomach.

One of our guys, Lenny, a real jokester, was dressed up like the rich, old lady, and kicked him in the groin. "That's for giving me crap money for my trinkets, buster."

Bert Z. went for his gun. Lenny chimed, "You wouldn't shoot an old lady, would ya?" Before Bert Z. knew what had happened, there were four other guns aiming at him and his sidekick. One was pointing directly at each of their heads. We relieved him and his sidekick of their guns and his load. He had twenty-four thousand dollars on him...cash. We shot his Caddie tires and split. We felt justified. They stood their dumbfounded.

There were repercussions for this. Turned out Bert Z. was connected. We were called down to the round table with Gendarmo's gang. Mario had been out of jail for a year now. I didn't know if he remembered me.

It was like being in courtroom without being sworn in. Gendarmo sat in the middle of a long table, flanked by armed bodyguards on both sides.

Me and Alex were on one side, the defendants; Bert Z. and his sidekick were on the other side, the plaintiffs. When Gerdarmo nodded at you, it was time to tell your story. No talking, you just knew to speak. I told my side, then Bert Z. told his side.

No jury. An intense silence. Then, like the harsh, no nonsense voice of Judge Judy only deeper, came a brief explanation. "Frankie, you were justified in doing what you did because the swag guy lied to you. Keep

243

the money, minus the court fees. Now both of you get out of here."

An irreversible decision, no court of appeals here. You are not supposed to hurt anybody that's in the mob and that includes cheating your fellow crooks. Although I was on the fringe, almost a wise guy, I was known from my early years and given a kind of waiver status. If someone's connected you are supposed to beef your complaints to the boss. The basic idea is, once there is violence or action taken without the boss knowing, everything shuts down. Then the underground loses money, and cops start to show up. That doesn't benefit anyone. I could have gotten in big trouble for taking the "justice" into my own hands. But I think Gerdarmo liked me. This was the second time he'd let me slide. The fallen angels were on my side.

Chapter Twenty-one

Every now and then my Catholic upbringing creeps into my mind and makes me reassess what I am doing. While I enjoyed figuring out the schemes and plots to these misguided adventures, I started thinking that I felt bad for the old lady that we took the money from. Even if she was game. I mean, what if the circumstances were different and she was really scared? What if that old lady was my mother?

I don't know, a moment of weakness would hit and I'd imagine that someday my mom would look down on me from heaven after having reviewed the big book and smack me on the head with a wooden spoon chucked from the skies above. There I would be walking in the street someday, and boom, out of nowhere a giant wooden spoon would crash down and knock me unconscious. Then I'd have a stupid scar like Eddie Finger. With these delusional thoughts in mind, I decided to stick with gambling.

Despite all my schemes, I was still working in construction. Alex, my instigator in crime and still bartender, told me about a guy named Bobby Dents, who had just gotten out of jail and needed a job. He was a nice enough guy so I hired him. He wasn't much of a laborer; he could handle a load, but he preferred brains to brawn. Like myself, he was always a man with a plan. I kept him on the payroll because I could see we would soon become partners.

I was looking to break into gambling big time. There were men who made their living gambling, and I wanted to join their ranks. With Bobby as my New York liaison, I took off for Vegas under the name of Flem Cusso, a New York trucking firm owner. I used that name 'cause I had a nice-looking diamond pinkie ring with the initials F.C. on it, and I wanted to wear it as a status symbol. I wasn't much into jewelry; in fact,

I lost half the stuff ever given to me, but this ring I had a special affection for. It also didn't hurt that there really was a trucking guy by the name of Flem Cusso, so if anyone looked him up in the yellow pages, it'd seem legit. You gotta admit, though, walking around with a first name like Flem takes a lot of courage.

I masterminded this elaborate scheme that took several months to establish. I always used Bobby as my Vegas partner or New York connection.

I would take a junket to Las Vegas and pose as Cusso. I went on a junket because everything is given to you for free if you are a gambler: food, plane fare, hotel bills, the works is all compted. They want to lure you into their web.

All I had to do was look like a big gambler. I wasn't really gambling at all. I would have somebody work with me and bet the opposites. The game of choice was craps. I would bet a thousand bucks and Bobby would bet a thousand against me. If I bet the come line, he'd bet don't come. If I won, I'd get my money from the casino; if I lost, Bobby got the money from the casino. Either way I couldn't lose, and it created an illusion of an endless stash of money. I built the reputation as a high roller.

Once my reputation was established, I started to be invited to all the casinos under the fictitious name of Flem Cusso. No one questioned that I was Flem. I would take good certified checks up to five thousand and cash them in at the casinos. At the same time, I was filing credit applications. After you do this five times and everything checks out, there's no question that you are cashing valid certified checks. I was known as a rounder, a person with solid credit.

To make this scam work, I had to build up my fake reputation by going to Vegas five or six times over a period of four months. I used to go and gamble in each hotel, giving them lots of action. On each trip I would check into three or four hotels at the same time. Each hotel would give me the plane fare and comp me for about seven hundred. I'd wind up having about three thousand with me from the hotels.

I had my original plane ticket, and each hotel would reimburse me for flying down. I also made additional money on each hotel, and this gave me the needed money to gamble. If any of the hotels had checked, it was legitimate that I, Flem Cusso, had flown down. They didn't know that I was checking in at other hotels, as well. I would give each hotel action and then fly back.

Now that I had built up credit in Vegas, I was also checking in at the Hilton Hotel in New York as Flem Cusso. After three months I opened a savings account at the Sterling National Bank of New York under the name of Cusso. Back then a person could open up a savings account with no ID. Today, they need your history, references, even your damn shoe size. I used the savings account to open up the checking account in New York.

Once the accounts were opened I went in for the big money. I gave the bank five thousand cash and they gave me a real certified check worth five thousand. Now I had a real certified check with real verifiable numbers on it. I would then make forged certified checks, ten forges of five thousand equaling fifty thousand using the same real numbers. That way if the hotel called up the bank to see if the certified number was real, there was a real number that matched. Only one was the real five-thousand-dollar certified check; the rest were forges, but the numbers checked out, so they didn't check the check itself. You got that?

Anyway, I flew out to the Dunes in Vegas on a weekend when the banks were closed, so they couldn't verify the checks.

I took the ten five-thousand-dollar checks and cashed them in at ten different casinos. Remember, one hotel had the real check. I would put the check into the casino's cashier. I would play a little, win or lose, and then I would cash in the rest. At some hotels I made a thousand; in some I lost a thousand. But in the end, I pulled from Caesars and MGM fifteen thousand dollars each, from the Hilton, Frontier, Sands and Dunes I got ten thousand dollars a piece, and from the Flamingo and Union Plaza an additional five thousand each. All in all, I dumped eighty-seven thousand dollars in bad checks. Not a bad days pay.

By Monday, when the banks were open and the checks could be verified, I was gone. When the checks began to bounce, the FBI was called in.

Agents searched everywhere looking for information on the crook but turned up sour. This went on for months. In the meantime, Bobby and I also dealt in certified check scams with diamonds and furs at exchange places. We used the same basic principal, gave a deposit by a real check, then, when we went to pick up the diamonds or furs, we would pay with a forged certified check, go after bank hours so they couldn't check it, and take the merchandise. Since the first check cleared, they trusted us on the second check. We did this to several stores.

Meanwhile, they were closing in on me on the Vegas scam and I didn't even know it. What did me in was a telephone call. They traced a phone call from the Sands Hotel that Bobby's wife had made to a public phone at the Eight Wonders on Queens Boulevard in New York.

The Feds started setting up tents and taking photos of every patron that went into the place. After hundreds of photos were gathered, they took the photos to the Vegas casinos and I was identified as the man posing as Flem Cusso.

Then they took that picture of me and brought it to the Eight Wonders and asked who I was, and of all people, that son of a bitch, no good rat bartender, Alex, squealed.

After that the rest was easy. They found out my name and where I lived. I was arrested and brought to the Federal House of Detention in lower Manhattan. I couldn't believe it. My first stint in jail. My most elaborate plan gone sour because of a stupid phone call, and Bobby's wife wasn't even supposed to be on the trip, but she'd begged to come. I tell you, it's a pretty broad every time.

I called Nellie and Deidra to let them know what had happened. Deidra was going to get money to bail me out. Nellie and I decided to tell the girls I went away on construction business and would be away for a while. I didn't want my girls knowing I was in jail.

I was sent to Vegas to be tried. I had a defense attorney assigned to me. I was facing up to sixty years in prison and was charged with seven counts of fraud by wire and interstate transport of forged securities.

It was a four-day trial, and I was convicted. It amazed me that my first thoughts were to look at this like a new adventure. Everything from being handcuffed, to general lockup, to being sentenced and witnessing my own trial. I was almost detached like I was in some movie. The public defender actually did a good job, I could have gotten twenty years, but instead I only got a one to three to run concurrently with Vegas.

I was sent to Sandstone Federal Prison in Minnesota. This was a rough prison, very strict. Temperatures reached forty below. But it got worse. I guess when it rains, it pours. When I got arrested for Vegas, they also got me on the diamond and fur scam. So I was sent back to New York to be tried on the stolen merchandise while I was serving time in Sandstone. Since we were prisoners, the first class treatment was out. You didn't fly there you were bused. A two and a half -month bus tour with pit stops in many jail cells along the way.

I missed my kids and thought about asking Nellie to bring the girls to see me since I was in New York, but then decided against it. I don't think seeing your dad in jail leaves a good impression on a kid. As adults we don't always think of the effects that our actions can have on our children. Not while we're doing it anyway. Hell, I was still a boy at heart. I loved the adventure, not the consequences. But like they say, don't do the crime if you can't do the time. The odd thing is all I ever wanted is what any father wants, to make a million bucks and give it to my daughters so they wouldn't have to depend on any one or ever struggle in their lives. Oh well, the best laid plans of mice and men.

While in New York, I was convicted on the fur scam. So after I did time in Sandstone, I had another engagement at Rikers to look forward to and then another six months up the river in Sing Sing.

Sing Sing was literally up the river from New York City, that's were they got the expression from. I was getting a U.S. tour of the penal system and checking in as a featured guest. The towels and the food sucked. Not much different from some airlines. Was it all worth it? It was all I knew.

After two months in Sandstone, thinking I was headed toward Rikers, the FBI played me like a ping-pong ball and took me back to Vegas again, this time to face a grand jury. They were sure I didn't act alone, which was kind of insulting. They wanted to know who else was in the scheme with me. I wouldn't rat on Bobby. Even if his birdbrain wife got me into this mess. I was true to my friends. Misplaced loyalty. I only know, do unto others as you would have others do unto you. I wouldn't tell for fear of a wise guy's karma. I envisioned some big fat wise guy Buddha with a cigar smiling and sounding like James Cagney, repeating, "Don't be a dirty rat see."

I refused to answer any questions at the grand jury trial. The way I saw it was, it's a lot more difficult to be a consistent liar than to tell the truth, so you might as well tell the truth or keep your mouth shut. I decided to keep my mouth shut. I was the speak-no-evil monkey. The prosecutor tried everything to get a name out of me.

"Mr. Crooks, did you work alone?" he asked.

"Yes."

"You had no one working with you?"

"No one."

"Who made the phone call?"

"I don't know."

"You don't know who made the phone call that got you in trouble?"

"I don't know."

"Then you were working with someone?"

257

"No."

"Why are you protecting someone who is going to let you rot in jail?"

I didn't answer.

"You are under oath. We know you worked with someone. We will find out who that person was. If you help us, you will be looked at in a better light." Then he leaned forward. "And it might shave time off your sentence."

I didn't answer.

"What was the name of the person that helped you in Vegas?"

"No one."

The judge intervened. "Mr. Crooks, you are instructed to cooperate with council.

"Your honor, maybe Mr. Crooks here needs some time in the local jail cell to think things over."

The frustrated prosecuting attorney suggested to the judge that the only way to force me to talk was to stop my time until I testified. The judge thought for a millisecond and agreed. Next case. The law will protect everybody who can afford to hire a good lawyer; unfortunately I was not in that situation. The judge stopped my federal time and put me in Clark County Jail.

Clark County Jail was a holding pen for those awaiting trial. Kind of like purgatory. I was to be held in Vegas until I agreed to testify against my partner. They wanted me to rat him out. Until I did, none of the days I spent there would count towards the completion of my sentence.

This really stunk. It was a battle of the wills. They had nothing to loose. I had only the days of my life counting towards wise guy karma, and I wasn't even a wise guy!

While I was in jail, I decided the best line of strategy was to keep a low profile, and make some friends. I even tried to make myself look a little crazy by wearing dark sunglasses in my cell as I was reading. They thought I was nuts.

You hear a lot of stories in jail...everything imaginable. If some writer wanted ideas, all they'd have to do is look up some crime stories, spend a few days with these guys, and they'd have all the information they needed for plots, motives, and people's passions. I mean, it's fascinating to see how the criminal mind works and how people justify their actions. I'm no exception.

I was put into a six-man cell. There was a Mexican, an Italian, two Spanish guys, a WASP, and myself. The whole freakin' United Nations was in there. The Mexican, Juan L., was in for mayhem; he'd stabbed somebody in the eye. His trial was coming up.

Juan L. got sent back to Mexico because he was illegal. In the meantime his girl started to live with this white guy. A few weeks later, Juan L. sneaked back to the States to get his girl. She was happy to see him and wanted to go back with him. The white guy came into the house and threatened to beat up Juan L., not believing the girl wanted to go with him. The guy came towards Juan L., and he panicked, knowing he was illegally there. Juan L. stabbed him in the eye and fled. The police found him five hours later. I told Juan L. to say that he and his girl were going to get married. The white guy was drunk, came into the house, and ran into the kitchen.

I gave him an alibi. I told him to say that he was making a sandwich and had a knife in his hand. The white guy came at you with a bat, you raised your hand to protect yourself, and the white guy ran into the knife. Damn, I would have made a good defense lawyer...move over Cochran.

Juan L. went to trial and beat the case. He was being held at Clarks County waiting for extradition back to Mexico because he was illegal. Juan L. was grateful. He said he would pay me back some day.

Whatever, I do things because I feel they're right at the time, not because I'm expecting payback. But like I said, it doesn't hurt to make friends.

I had been at Clark for a month by that time, still refusing to testify and name Bobby in the two scams. I thought I'd rot in there. That's when a riot broke out.

Chapter Twenty-two

Most riots start the same way. Someone feels they are being treated unfairly, the chants grow louder, the crowds grow restless, people are frustrated, and like one giant blob, they attack and devour everything in sight. It's like one giant mind takes over. I think they call it group consciousness, or some fancy name like that.

This riot started because the guards put a black preacher's son into a cell with two white supremacists. Whether it was planned or not, who knows. The white guys put a sheet up, blocking the view from the other inmates. But you can't block sound. They stabbed the black kid and the blood splattered onto the sheet. The black guy's curdling screams echoed out while he was being stabbed. They killed the guy. Everyone heard it.

Other guards came in, and other than taking him out the back, they paraded his bloodied body through the corridor where everyone could see. I don't care, black, white, red or purple, it was wrong.

It was recreation time, so no one was locked up. An eerie silence fell over the place. Like a skin boil ready to break through to the surface, I sensed trouble coming. I got together the people that I knew, the white guys that I had befriended, and went to my cell. It was survival. At this point it was only color—not involvement—that mattered. The anger was aimed at the white race, not the guilty parties. Even the black guys that I had made friends with had to watch out for their own hides. We made whatever weapons we could to protect ourselves.

Meanwhile, the blacks were jamming cell doors so they couldn't close. They were beating and stabbing any white inmates in their path. They were dragging some out of their cells and kicking them senseless on the floors.

We knew our time would come and we were ready. Every time rioters came to look into our cell, no one would enter, because there were six of us ready to pounce on anyone who entered first. And the way the doors were jammed, only one person could enter at a time. All the other white inmates got beat up. We stood our ground.

In the meantime, the guards went into the middle of the jail in an area where they could lock themselves off, be protected from the rioters, control the gates, call for reinforcements, and observe the whole thing.

They'd seen the six of us in our cell. They told us to get out of our cell and go to the end of the corridor where there was a double gate. They told us they would open the gate and let us out into a safe area.

The guards were about a hundred feet to the right of our cell, and the double gates were about two hundred and fifty feet in the other direction. There was no way the guards were going to let us in with them for

265

fear we'd hold them as hostages, or worse turn them over to the angry rioters.

But there wasn't much choice. We either had to trust the guards who hated us or deal with the angry rioters. We couldn't hold the cell all night. We made the only move we could. We waited till we felt we could make a break. Quickly we exited the cell, then formed a circle to protect our backs. As one unit, with weapons in hand, we tried to reach the end of the hallway where the gate hopefully would open. If not, we were dead men.

Not even twenty feet outside our cell, about fifteen blacks came out and stood in between us and the gate. They just stood there as if daring us to come any farther. For a moment we debated our choice: to fight or head back to our cell and hope for the best. We decided to fight our way through.

Just then, out of some jail cells in between where the blacks were and us, the Mexicans jumped in with

Juan L. at the lead. He said, "I told you I wouldn't let you down. I don't forget." Juan L. whistled, and behind the blacks came a group of about thirty-five Mexicans. Now the blacks were surrounded on both sides by Mexicans. Juan L. yelled, "Let these six guys through, man. They did nothin'. Otherwise you have to fight all them plus my compadres." No one said nuthin'. The air was tense. Slowly, with Juan L. surrounding us, the Mexican gang led us through the sea of angry faces. They helped us get to the end of the hall and to the double doors, keeping our attackers at knife's distance.

We got to the double doors. We waited, praying the freakin' gates would open. Then came the load unlock crank. At that sound all the rioters started screaming and running towards the doors. The doors slid open just wide enough for one person to get through. I let the other guys go through first. The Mexicans detained them long enough for me to slide through the door.

The guards quickly closed the door. I heard pounding and screaming on the other side. The Mexicans and the blacks didn't battle it out. Juan L. probably saved my life. Now we were even.

The guards took us through another set of doors and into the kitchen. There were about fifty people scattered about. It looked like a butcher shop, with so much blood all over the floors, guys with their necks sliced, ears half dangling, gore and guts that would top any B movie list. They took us to the hospital in handcuffs. I wasn't hurt, but I claimed my back was injured just to get the hell out of the jail for a while.

The nurses tended our wounds with curiosity. Probably trying to figure out which ones of us were murderers and rapists. Wondering whether they should follow their Hippocratic Oath and help us, or let us bleed to death as the scum of society. I wasn't scum. I was just a guy scamming and making a buck. I would beat the shit out of a rapist, drug dealer or child molester myself.

After this incident, that left one guard and five inmates dead, the court ruled the Clark County Jail wasn't safe for federal prisoners. They sent me back to Sandstone, where my time started again. A few bruises and I never had to squeal. Some horrible incidents in a weird way disguise themselves as blessings. This was one of those times.

Chapter Twenty-three

Two years later, after I got out of jail and since I didn't rat on Bobby, he felt he owed me one. While I was in jail, he had sent money to Nellie and the girls to make sure they didn't starve. In the meanwhile he opened up a place called "Johnny's Jersey City" in Manhattan with his share of the money from the Vegas scam. He made me his combination night manager/bouncer.

The place was a starting ground for many of today's famous bands. The likes of Bruce Springstein and many hot bands begged to play at our place. We'd charge them, and they'd bring a crowd. Everybody was happy. It was the "in" place.

With a few drinks in them, boys get pretty brazen. They have this male ego need to show off for their female counterparts. We had to keep them in line.

I guess 'cause Bobby never went to jail, he still had his hands in illegal things. As for me, I guess I didn't learn my lesson or rather I learned my lesson, and now thought I was too smart to get caught again. With this thinkin' I got involved with Bobby in a stolen bond deal. What can I tell ya, I got a hard head. If my moma, God rest her soul, knew she'd kick my ass.

I went back to hanging out at Eight Wonders and the same old gang was there. Alex, the bartender, was gone. Good thing for him because I would have had to beat the shit out of him for squealing.

The gang was glad to see me. It was like a homecoming party, without pictures. It's not like people are going to ask you, "What you been up to?" For Christ's sake, they knew I was in jail for a few years. It's not a picnic. I played it off as all tough guys do. I had my war stories and made them into funny tales. But really, who the hell wants to be locked up like a tiger in the zoo? Being told when to eat shit and sleep. It's the price you pay.

There was this guy at Eight Wonders named Mel. He owned a hair-cutting place called "Gents Only." Which was kind of odd since he wore a bad toupee and was no gentleman. He was a little guy, about five foot three and wore pants that you would only see on a golf course. He had a wide, long nose, and beady eyes, and a pot belly. He was no looker. But he knew how to schmooze. It amazes me how schmoozing and joking can always make a person more attractive, no Robert Redford, but more attractive. Actually still more amazing was the fact that Mel thought he was good-looking. He would comment how any girl that turned him down was an idiot for losing out on such a catch. He meant it. Even I wasn't that conceited. But that gave him the courage to approach the knockouts. He was never discouraged by a woman saying "no." An ego of steel that guy had.

Mel was a Jewish bookmaker who liked to hangout with us Italians. To me the two are so similar anyway—the overprotective dominant mothers and strong family ties. Plus both love a sense of humor, and that I think that is the biggest bond between the two cultures. Anyway, he was heavy into the bookmaking. We became friends.

I had money stashed away and put up ten thousand dollars Yankee money, which is wise guy talk for I bet ten thousand dollars on the Yankees. If I "lay it off," give it to another bookmaker, the bookmaker works on a fifty percent win.

To understand the self-thought genius of my next scam, which ultimately lead to the biggest heist of all time, you have to know how bookmakers work.

A bookmaker calls his "action," all the bets, into a bookmaking house. A bookmaking house is just a person with a phone that you call and put in all your bets to. Each house is set up for about a week. At the end of the week, the house tallies up all the winning and losing bets. If the bettors lose, the bookmaker and the house split the profits. For example, let's say a person bets a hundred bucks, the bookmaker would keep fifty and the house would keep fifty. Simple enough. Basic math.

If the bettor wins, the house gives the bookmaker the hundred bucks to pay the bettor, but the bookmaker has to work himself out of the hole. Meaning if the bettor wins the hundred before the bookmaker wins any money, that's no good. The bookmaker has got to win over a hundred bucks to cover himself. It gets easier once you do it, kind of like algebra.

I came up with a scheme. I told Mel to place the bets the opposite of whatever the bettor told him to do. If they say a hundred bucks on one team, you bet on the opposite team and call that bet into the house. This way the house is paying you even if you lose. Then you just never pay back the house.

I became partners with Mel. He placed the bets. I'd collect on them. We wound up with a lot of money. Sometimes I had to chase the bettors down. Remember this wasn't the honor roll society.

One of the bettors, Moe, worked at Kennedy Airport for Lufthansa. He had made a sizable bet into another bookmaker and didn't get paid even though he won. He came to Mel to see if he could help him.

Mel came to me and asked me if I would go down and speak to the bookmaker for the bettor. In my persuasive way, I got Moe's money for him, with interest.

The grateful Moe went to Mel and gave him a little inside information. He told Mel about large shipments of gold that were coming in from Lufthansa. He said he knew exactly when they were coming in. Mel passed on the information to me. Always one to take on a challenge, I told him I would set everything up. I set to masterminding the deal of all deals. I told Mel we had to wait for a phone call before going ahead with any plans. We had to get the right players in place. Anxiously we waited for the call.

Unfortunately or fortunately depending how you look at it, I had in the meantime sold Bobby's stolen bonds for him. The guy we sold them to got caught and ratted me out. No one has integrity anymore! I went to jail for a second time, in Danbury, Connecticut. Bobby again was off the hook. I think it was time to reassess my friends.

While I was in jail the phone call came through, and I wasn't around to take it. Anxious Mel went to somebody else that he had no prior history with. In something this size you have to know the players. Mel thought it was enough that Moe had the plan.

They had four guys, sacks, and three gunman. They stole a truck, cut a lock, and went through the conveniently unguarded gate into the Lufthansa terminal. Then they went into the security area and overtook the planted guard that was there. The plant gave up all the gold and stuff. He was in.

Mel got anxious after the heist was done that he wasn't getting his share of the money. So he leaned on the powers that be, and they leaned on him by throwing him out of a plane for pressuring them. The other four involved were killed as well.

Everything was set up by Moe. He had the eyes to know how it would work since he had been at Kennedy for years. Moe was the informant with all the details. He knew everything down to the number of rats onboard.

It was an easy setup, but nobody was supposed to touch the money for six months, the cooling off period. Patience is not a virtue shared by many tough guys. Loads of money gets real itchy in inpatient hands. Big ticket items like new cars, furs and boats are easy to trace. Those with loose wallets make it bad on the others. Temptation leads to carelessness, which leads to bragging rights, which leads to the only way to shut them up...death.

Chapter Twenty-four

While I was in jail I made friends with a guy named Pete. Pete showed me how to make a buck...literally—by counterfeiting. Everybody wanted to know his method. His bills were known to be among the best replicas. But like Colonial Sanders the recipe was a secret. He told me what he did, but not how. Pete would get one dollar bills and take off all their ink. Then he would use the government-issued paper and reprint hundreds on them. Using the same paper made the quality and feel of the counterfeits seem real and therefore harder to detect. It was artwork. Okay, it was copying artwork, just like any artist does till he develops his own style.

I wanted my own style or trademark. While in prison, I took advantage of their work programs by learning the printing trade. These programs are designed to rehabilitate you by giving you a skill to go back into society with. It rarely worked. It was knowledge and fodder for other crimes. In this case I learned to perfect my printing technique. Now I had the basics of printing and the knowledge that something could be done. When I got out, it took me almost seven months to find the formula to clean dollar bills without a trace. Like any good scientist, I learned through trial and error.

I was now living with Bobby in Long Island with jail sentence number two behind me. I lived in the basement of his house. I told Bobby about the counterfeiting but wouldn't give him the formula. As always, he was in. Never one to pass up an opportunity...especially when it came to money, even if it was money we literally were making.

It became routine: I would clean the bills, then make them with my special formula. My own moneymaking homemade recipe. Bobby put up the money for the printing machine and camera. I gave him fifty percent of what we made, but he wasn't satisfied. Greed is one of the seven deadly sins that constantly surround wannabe wise guys.

You know they say money is the root of all evil, I believe lack of money is the root, or at least the perceived lack causes a lot more headaches. He wanted to make the bills faster, spend them faster. Fast, in certain things, can lead to carelessness. Carelessness in any profession leads to no good. The principles of perfection work in both the good and evil, you just have to decide where to use them.

Bobby went to Atlantic City and cashed in thirty thousand dollars of phony bills in one shot. They caught him. What the hell was he thinking? Why not wear a sign on the back of his shirt saying, "Arrest me." Bobby went to jail and this time, he didn't squeal on me. But by getting arrested and sentenced he also left me with no machinery or merchandise because it was confiscated. That's the way of the world. I get caught, he's still in business. He gets caught, they take my tools. Some luck. It's like the big hand of God coming down and saying, "You've been a bad boy, Frankie. Now give me your toys."

I learn my lessons hard. Being the resourceful man that I am, I found a way to get the money to buy my own machine. This time I decided blood was thicker than water and went into a "family business" with my cousins Jerry and David, who seemed to have trotted down the same crooked path that I had chosen—without my help.

Jerry and David were in Florida at the time. I went up to see David, who had just gotten out of the service with an honorable discharge. Innocently, they asked what I was up to. I told them straight. I don't know if it was the fact that their cousin was doing it that intrigued them, or that it was a quick way to make a buck or the thrill of living on the edge, but whatever it was they both wanted in. No one in the family knew they were getting involved. I'm sure they wouldn't have approved. But although they were my younger cousins, they were adults, too. Everyone is in charge of their own destiny. I gave them a choice, they chose "yes." There would have been no hard feelings either way.

We set up an operation in Florida with David running it. I would come down to make sure everything was going okay. Things were going good. I was satisfied with the three to four hundred dollars a day we was making. Like in any job there are good samples and bad ones. You discard the inferior quality ones and only sell the good merchandise to your customers. In this business the irregulars couldn't just go down to Filene's Basement at some discounted price. The irregulars or misfits could cost us our freedom. I would give them to David to destroy.

Unbeknownst to me, David kept them and would sneak them out of the office. Then he'd use them. Bad artwork is easy to spot. I mean for Christ's sake, on some of them Franklin's eyes were crossed. The jerk acted as if I was throwing away real money. Some of the bills were blurry. A blind person could have spotted them without Braille or a dog.

The weird thing was David was totally surprised when he got caught. He'd all but put on a sign saying, "Illegal bills made here...come and get them!" He obviously went to the same school as Bobby Dents.

Anyway, so David got caught, panicked, and squealed on me and Jerry. Not only that, he set us up so he could negotiate for less time for himself in prison.

He called us and said we needed to come to Florida, that there was trouble. His voice sounded weird. I had a gut feeling that things weren't right. We drove slowly by the office, and the lights were out. I sent Jerry to go pick up the machinery from our office and put it in a truck to hide it. He was supposed to follow me back to New York. The FBI caught him on the road, opened the truck, and he was caught red-handed.

Since I was driving a car I was faster and made it back to New York. But I wasn't fast enough, 'cause the FBI was waiting at my apartment and once again I was personally escorted to jail in silver bracelets.

David, the squealer, didn't get off like he thought he would. All three of us went to jail. But they split the family unit. I went to jail in New York, and they served time in Florida. After a few months I was transferred to Lewisburg, Pennsylvania.

When I was put in jail for the third time, I just looked around and said, "What a fine mess you got yourself into, Frankie...mmm...mmmm...mmm." I'm too old for this shit. Who the hell wants to be a three-time loser? When you're own cousin rats you out, what shot have you got? But it was my own fault. I should have never gotten them involved. A man's gotta take his own blame.

My sister found out about it, since she read it in the paper. She reamed me out for involving the family, "Frankie, you think you're some kind of wise guy, you're not. Smarten up already. Use that brain of yours for something else. I don't like what you did, but you know I still love ya." She eventually forgave me. No one ever mentioned my brother Vinny.

My brother Joey never condemned me, but he tried to talk sense into me, too. I was disappointed and embarrassed. It was a catch-22, and I wasn't willing to catch anymore. While I was in Lewisburg for one and a half years, I vowed to go straight. I didn't make a good criminal. Who knows, maybe with all the psychology crap, if I ever looked into it, maybe I wanted to get caught to have my decision made for me. I doubt it, but it's a possibility.

I think Nellie and my kids had enough of visiting me in penitentiaries, too. Especially since Nellie didn't drive and her new husband, Lucifer—that name alone should have told her something—was this one-armed hillbilly wacko from West Virginia who would always tease the girls about visiting me in prison. He would tell them to bake me a cake with a file in it, or on the way up in the car he'd play "Jailhouse Rock," until Nellie yelled at him to turn it off. They hated the guy, and frankly I have no clue, nor did anyone else, what Nellie saw in him. Maybe he had a good insurance policy.

The girls would beg me to be good so I could get out sooner on good behavior. It was heartbreaking. They even wrote letters to the judge saying that I was not a bad guy, and could the judge go easy on their dad, because after all, "he didn't kill anyone"? If it was only that easy...

My oldest daughter, Frannie, picked up my survival tactic of humor. She became a standup comic and started making jokes about it. She once sent me a joke that she wrote about me: "My dad's in jail. Sometimes my mom forgets and threatens us with it when we're bad. 'Wait till your father gets home.' Ma, he's doin' three to five...For Christmas I don't get gifts, but I'm the only kid on the block with ten sets of license plates." She told me it went well in front of some audiences, but the classier places felt they needed to take up a hat collection for her, give her counseling, or offer her some hot chocolate.

My younger one, Sherry, was just out and out disappointed in me. She didn't understand how I could like spending time in jail better than finding out a way to stay out so I could spend more time with them. How do you explain that one?

I was disappointed myself. I liked the excitement that crime offered; it made me feel I was getting away with something, but obviously if I kept getting caught, I wasn't. I didn't even make a good crook. Frannie suggested I take up bungee jumping instead if I needed the adrenaline rush that bad.

I guess she was right. When I say "kids don't try this at home" I mean it. First of all, you can't be a counterfeiter like I was today because they have the threads that run the entire length of the bill. All the good counterfeits are being made in other countries. Why not? They make better cars, why not our money? The same people who make the money for the government make it for other people in other countries, too. It's all in the machinery. They sell the printing machinery to other countries so naturally other governments have the ability to reproduce our bills.

Highly sophisticated computers are used to counterfeit. The small-time counterfeiter is out of business. It's the end of the world as we know it. So you have to learn to adjust.

289

Chapter Twenty-five

While I was in prison, two things happened that brought home the importance of my freedom. My brother Vinny died of a heart attack, and my best friend Mark died in a car crash. Being a prisoner, I wasn't allowed to go to either funeral. That broke my heart. I wanted to bend those metal bars like superman and break through the walls. You never know how much you miss your freedom till you can't pay your last respects. When people are alive you always think there's time later to spend with them. Then when they die, you realize just how valuable all your time is. I sure as hell didn't want to spend the rest of my time staring at a filthy toilet and cement wall.

Chapter Twenty-six

The last place I was sent to before I got out was like a camp. It was even called Camp McGregor. Our jobs were to take care of the local parks and keep the streets clean. It was like a country club. They even told you, "If you want to go home, there's the road." They said, "No one will stop you. But when we catch you, you get a minimum of five years added onto your sentence." We were all too close to getting out to chance it. It was like invisible shackles. That's freedom. You can have that soon, if you don't blow it.

At the camp we even did a bit of fire fighting for the community. It felt good to help the people. One time we even saved some local town folks who had fallen in the river. We became heroes...isn't it ironic.

When I came out of jail for the last time, I smelled the freedom. I had kept my mind sharp. I studied and got my high school equivalency and became a chess champion at McGregor. I loved chess, figuring out all the strategies and trying to guess your opponent's moves or force them into a corner. You have to look at all the options with chess. I also mastered bridge. As with everything else I had my own bridge system. A set of signals with my partner that were opposite of what they really meant. I would never cheat, 'cause I hated cheaters, but I would always try to devise a new method to play by. In some circles, they call that thinking outside the box. In others, they call it breaking the rules. I guess it depends on whose dealing the cards.

Anyway, as soon as I got out I did two things. I took my girls out to this old-fashioned ice cream parlor called "Jahn's" for this big dish called the Kitchen Sink. Thirty scoops of ice cream with every topping you could imagine. They should have served Pepto Bismol with it, 'cause we stuffed ourselves like pigs and had to be rolled out of there. We talked and recited some of the poems I had taught them since they were little like, "I wish I was a bird flyin' high up in the sky and if I saw you I'd go, ploop, right in your eye" or my other favorite, "I wish I was a tree, oops a dog just peed on me." To me that was the ultimate in positive thinking.

After I dropped them off, I made up for lost time with my girlfriend Deidra, who believe it or not, stuck by me through thick and thin. We didn't want to get married or nothin', but we had fun with each other. Besides, I was getting to old to fart around in nightclubs, especially these days when who knows what diseases you might pick up.

I also went back to Eight Wonders. Habits die hard, but I had learned my lesson...finally. I never wanted to go back to the loneliness of jail and not having loved ones around who I could trust.

I met an older union guy named Izzy over a scotch. He was tall, had gray hair, and was bent over slightly at the shoulders. I told him I was in the construction business and he asked me to do him a favor. To build a locksmith shop for him. In exchange he gave me money and showed me how to become a locksmith. I was proud of that shop. I did it from scratch all by myself. It felt good to be building something useful again.

Things seemed like they would work out okay after all. I picked up some odd jobs and learned to enjoy my family and friends more.

There were temptations along the way, no doubt, but I managed to avoid them. Like when Nellie's husband Lucifer asked me if I had the balls to go into a stolen car theft ring with him. I wanted to punch the jerk, but no one looks good sluggin' a one-armed man. The guy was a drunken fool, and more times than not, for the sake of Nellie and the kids, I pulled the bastard out of a bad situation. He was a liar, too, and I can't stand someone who always seems to be on the wrong side of the facts.

We stayed clear of each other after that, and eventually he and Nellie divorced, after he forged her name to some documents and was caught running two sets of books on his antique business. He wound up leaving Nellie $250,000 in the hole, and he nearly lost her the house. The IRS had a grand jury indictment after him. Last I heard he married some floozy who was in on some shady deals with him and moved into her parents house.

As for me, all I ever wanted to do was make my mark in this world. If I couldn't do it one way, I headed the other. I had justified it to myself, since I never hurt an individual, only casinos, banks, big business, and the government, that I was like some modern day Robin Hood.

I never stuck up a person, or personally robbed a person of what he worked for. I was a working man myself.

If I had to do it all over again I would go for education, 'cause most of my trouble came from lack of education. I think if I had learned my economic lessons and other things like that instead of trying to be a wise guy, I would have found a way to make a million dollars legit. Either way you can make money, but doing it the wrong way there's always the reality of jail.

Both my girls went to college, and I'm damn proud of it. Nellie did a good job keeping those kids straight and honest. She also drilled into them that nothing was impossible.

I tried to teach them what I could, but fatherhood wasn't easy. I tried to pass on some pearls of wisdom to them like, "You can just as easily fall in love with a rich man as a poor man." But they thought I was shallow and didn't understand love. I told them, "Don't worry, ninety percent of what you worry about won't come true anyway," but they still cried. I even told them to "love your enemies, but if you really want to make them mad ignore them," but they had a hard time with that one, too.

I did try to pass on my cooking skills to them, but they took after Nellie and the microwave became their best friend.

I even tried to help them make some money on the side. I told Frannie once that she should take out an ad in one of those penny savers that said, "Want Free Living? Try government subsidized housing. Free room and board. Light work load. Send five dollars for information." Then I told her that when the people sent in the money, you write back, "Commit a crime, go to jail." She refused to do it. No one appreciated my way of thinking.

I don't know what you think about me, but basically I think I'm a good guy who did some not so great things. I really do love my kids, and I enjoy having a good time. The weird thing is I always believed in God too. I asked him to guide me, and I think sometimes sending me to jail was his way of saying, "Straighten out, you hard-headed son." I'm glad Jesus was around, too, since I think without him I wouldn't have a shot of getting into heaven. I've asked the Big Man many times to forgive me. I've forgiven my cousin for ratting on me, and he forgave me for getting him into the trouble in the first place.

Through it all, I think my strongest asset was my sense of humor. I know I passed that onto my eldest daughter because she became not only a comic, but a comedy writer as well. She had a son, my first grandson, Matthew, and he has a quick wit, too. It's in the genes.

My youngest daughter speaks several languages, probably so she doesn't have to explain the things I did in English.

So why am I telling you all of this now? Why did I feel the need to pour out my heart to you, after I've been straight for a good twenty-five years? Because of two things. My grandson the other day asked me to tell him about my childhood. I've been teaching that kid the important things in life like fishing, kite flying, magic tricks, how to use a hammer and throw a good punch, how to fart on command, okay and I did throw in a math lesson or two by teaching him dice and the spread points in a game of football, but regardless...we grew real close. I tried to teach him my pearls of wisdom, too, like never argue with a woman, it's a losing battle, and that every man has three wishes in life; to outsmart the government, women, and fish. I even taught him the song, "Friendship"...you know the one that goes, "If you're ever in a jam, here I am. If you're ever up a tree, call on me. It's friendship, friendship..." We sing that every time we are together.

The bottom line is there's no way I want to let him know I was ever a crook. He looks up to me. I think it's the first time someone really needed me. Then I started thinkin' there was no way I could change the past, but possibly I could help the future.

You see, as I'm telling you this story, the angel of death has called upon me. It's not that I'm afraid of death, to me the people that are afraid of death are usually the same ones that are afraid of life. And it's not that I'm lookin' for any sympathy, because I'm not going through anything that anybody else isn't going to face someday. To me your body is like an old coat. When you die you take off that coat, but you still live on. The problem is, where exactly do you live on? Cancer is what got me. And once again it was my own fault, smoking two packs a day. I even beat cancer twice, and did I stop? No! I started smokin' again. We already know how thick my head is. I stopped this third time when Matthew gave me a lecture on secondhand smoke and told me he wanted me around when he grew up. How could I refuse the kid? But it was too late.

Even with that I tried to joke around. When I was getting the chemo, I had Frannie buy a Chia pet to see whose hair would grow back faster. I kept cutting its hair so I would win. Okay, so I hedged my bet a little. I just didn't want any heaviness around my death. Especially with Matthew around to see it.

You see, I've been staying at Frannie's house the last few months on hospice. The whole gang, Nellie, Sherry, Frannie and even Matthew have been helping me out. I gotta tell ya, it's pretty embarrassing for a tough guy to wear a diaper. And trying to play a good game of pool with one is nearly impossible!

The hospice people from Cabrini, though, were really nice. They have all these people coming over to help ya. Music therapists, nurses, nuns, and delivery boys who come and personally deliver your medicine to the door. I've never been so catered to in my life! This is what a king must feel like. Although I'd rather have my health, I'm not used to just sittin' around.

Recently, though, something happened that at least made me know I was still thinking. A delivery boy came by and was buzzing the bell. Nobody was home and I needed my pain medicine. It was really hard to walk by this point, but I needed that damn medicine and I was in Frannie's apartment on the third floor. I couldn't walk down the stairs and for some reason there was this rule that the boy couldn't come up with it. I took my cane, opened the glass door that lead to the balcony, and yelled for the kid to wait. I looked around, spotted a basket, tied it to a string, and lowered it down. I had him put the medicine in the basket. It was a struggle, but I hauled it back up. I guess my mind will work like this till the day I die.

The one thing that was really comforting in the last few weeks, though, was that I had a priest come over regularly from the local parish. I felt I had a lot to confess. The one thing I was never able to figure out about the church, though, was why they looked down on all forms of gambling except bingo and marriage.

I did figure out why people pray so much when they get older. It's like cramming for your finals. You know you are going to see the big man, and you're hoping that last-minute study can rack you up a few extra points. I'm not sure if it will work, but I'm betting on it.

Frannie told me about this psychic guy, John Edward, who apparently can speak to people once they crossover to the other side. She told me to write this guy's name down, since I have a habit of mixing things up. I don't want to be talking through some guy, Edward John and find out he's a plumber. She's going to contact me and find out how the trip went. If I'm vacationing in a hot humid climate or sitting around on a green golf course playing cards with my pals.

Anyway, I was thinkin' if I could lead some people away from crime by having them learn by my examples then maybe I would have made my mark on the world. So this was my shot. Look, I'm no Billy Graham. All I'm saying is believe in yourself no matter what you wind up doing and do the best you can. Life allows us to ask for what we want, but usually gives us what we deserve. Oh yeah, and always keep your sense of humor. Life is ten percent what you make it, and ninety percent on how you take it. You'll be a lot better off it you make the best of the best, and the least of the worst.

I know if I'd ever lost my sense of humor, I would have ended it a long time ago. I found ways to laugh through sickness, fights, breakups, and jail. Laughter, no matter who you are, heals. It's Gods way of saying "Hey you jerks, I created you and you get yourselves into some really fine messes. But I'll give you the choice. You can either laugh about it or cry...either way it will still happen...you'll just have a different take on the situation."

The bottom line is, with a sense of humor you can get through anything, including almost being a wise guy.

THE END

Fran Capo

Epilogue

The character of Frankie Crooks was based on an actual person. When Frankie died, he requested people to retell funny tales of his life. As promised, nothing but laughter was heard at his funeral.

To speak to Frank directly you must contact John Edward.

Fran did and Frankie joked with her about this book.

Fran Capo

Check out Fran Capo's other books:

To order simply circle the amount and put a check next to the item you want.

How to Get Publicity Without a Publicist: (An easy step by step guide to getting yourself in the newspapers, on radio and TV)
$20.00 U.S. /$23.00 Can   **Check here to order**

From building a dynamite press kit to developing a catchy hook, and the differences of how to do a radio interview as opposed to a TV interview, this book will guide you and prepare you to deal with reporters, and all aspects of the media to get the highest exposure possible for you or your business.

The Humor Approach: A Guide to Humor in Speaking.
$20.00 U.S. / $23.00 **Check here to order**
Can

Learn the tricks that the professionals use to add punch to your presentations. This book will show you the pitfalls to avoid when using humor, tips on how to make a joke funnier, delivery techniques, when to use humor and how to select the appropriate humor for each occasion. Whether you're a teacher, a corporate executive, a lawyer, fundraiser, or a salesman, this book will help you add sparkle to your speech.

How to Break into Voiceovers: An Itty Bitty Guide to Big Business
$20.00/U.S. / $23.00 Can   **Check here to order**

___

Learn how to: get a dynamite demo tape, audition, get an agent, get your first job, and look professional your first time out. Complete with interviews from agents, producers and editors.

It Happened in New York (TwoDot Books, an imprint of Falcon Publishing)
ISBN I-56044-899-7
$9.95 U.S. / $12.00 Can   **Check here to order**

___

Thirty true fascinating events that helped make New York what it is today, told with a comedic yet dramatic flair. Read about the purchase of Manhattan from the wrong set of Indians; how Woodstock started as a sitcom idea; the world's greatest hoax; how they turned off Niagara Falls, and much more!
Plus a trivia section.

Audio Tapes Available:
Fran's Fast Fractured Fairy Tales
Check here to order ___
$10.00 U.S. /$12.00 Can
A collection of modern day, humorous, sarcastic bedtime stories told at the speed of light by The World's Fastest Talking Female.

Look for Fran's upcoming books:

Adrenaline Adventures: Dream it, Read it, Do it. (Due out in 2002)
Fran's personal stories about extreme adventures to motivate, inform, and entertain the reader. Experience and learn where to bungee jump, fly combat aircraft, go panning for gold, scuba dive with sharks, drive racecars, and much more.

It Happened in New Jersey (The Globe-Pequot Press) (Due out in 2003)
Follow up to the successful It Happened in New York, this book details, thirty true fascinating events that shaped the state of New Jersey. Learn about the ghosts that swindled money out of Morristown residents, the first true terrorist attack on the United States, the fight of the century and much more. Plus a special trivia section.

To order your autographed copy of any of the above items:

You can either order online through Paypal @ www.francapo.com or copy this page, check desired items and send this coupon and a check or money order to:

Fran Capo
P.O. Box 272
Flushing, NY 11358
To learn about and see a video of Fran Capo's corporate events, lectures, articles, stand-up, cybersitcom and booking information go to www.francapo.com or e-mail Fran at FranCNY@aol.com